Before It's Too Late

Latrese N. Carter

URBAN
Renaissance

www.urbanbooks.net

Urban Books, LLC
78 East Industry Court
Deer Park, NY 11729

Before It's Too Late Copyright © 2010 Latrese N. Carter

ISBN 13: 978-1-60162-222-8
ISBN 10: 1-60162-222-8

First Printing August 2010
Printed in the United States of America

10 9 8 7 6 5 4 3 2 1

This is a work of fiction. Any references or similarities to actual events, real people, living, or dead, or to real locales are intended to give the novel a sense of reality. Any similarity in other names, characters, places, and incidents is entirely coincidental.

Distributed by Kensington Publishing Corp.
Submit Wholesale Orders to:
Kensington Publishing Corp.
C/O Penguin Group (USA) Inc.
Attention: Order Processing
405 Murray Hill Parkway
East Rutherford, NJ 07073-2316
Phone: 1-800-526-0275
Fax: 1-800-227-9604

Hom

HACKNEY LIBRARY SERVIC

Please return this book to any library in Hackney,
before the last date stamped. Fines may be charged if .
Avoid fines by renewing the book (subject to it NOT being reserve

Call the renewals line on 020 8356 2539

People who are over 60, under 18 or registered disabled
are not charged fines.

H, A, B   09/12

⊖Hackney

Prologue

Janice Prescott (Mama)

I was startled by the rapid pounding on my front door. I quickly sat up and glanced at the clock. It read 1:30 A.M. *Who in the world is knocking on my door this time of morning?*

I hurriedly threw on my bathrobe and slippers. Panicky, I almost tripped running down the stairs. I looked through the peephole and saw two men dressed in police uniforms. I knew something was wrong.

Slowly, I opened the door just enough to stick my head through it. "Yes? May I help you?" My voice quivered as I spoke.

"Good morning, Ma'am. I'm so sorry to wake you. I'm Officer Chesney," he said showing his police badge. "And this is Officer Kinny."

"Are you Janice Prescott?" Officer Kinny asked after he flashed his badge.

"Y-y-yes," I responded, nervously. "Why?"

"Ma'am, do you mind if we come in?"

Confused and scared, I was hesitant about letting the gentlemen into my home. Police officers don't usually show up at a person's home at such a time unless they've come to deliver bad news. "Officers," I said as I stepped aside to allow them into my living room. "It's 1:30 A.M. Can y'all please tell me why you're here this time of morning? I can tell by the gloomy looks on your faces, something's wrong. So, please, just tell me."

"Ma'am, do you know Tori and Dani Prescott?"

"Yes, I do. They're my daughters. Why? Has something happened to them?"

"Well there's been an accident, and I need to know if you can describe the car your daughter Tori drives and if possible, her keys," Officer Chesney said with a dismal facial expression.

My mind was clouded. The officers' presence alone was enough to make me nervous, and coupled with the kind of questions they asked, this only made me feel worse. At first, I couldn't picture Tori's car, but then the color quickly flashed in my head. "Tori drives a forest green Toyota Camry," I responded, sounding unsure. "And I don't know what all is on her car keys, but I do know she has a cross keychain with the name of our church, Brice Memorial Baptist Church, written in blue letters."

"Are you sure, Ma'am?"

"I'm sure," I answered, agitated. I needed them to hurry up and get to the point. "Why? Why are you asking me to describe my daughter's car? Has something happened to my girls?" My voice trembled.

Officer Chesney reached in his pocket and pulled out what appeared to be Tori's keys. My eyes immediately noticed the cross keychain. My heart fell into my stomach.

"Mrs. Prescott, I'm so sorry to tell you that your daughters have been in a terrible accident on northbound I-95," he said. "The Maryland Department of Transportation is still investigating, but it seems that your daughters pulled over on the shoulder of the road. We're not sure why as of yet. It seems, while they were parked, a pick-up truck, speeding about 100 miles per hour slammed into the Toyota Camry when the driver lost control. The impact caused the car to flip over several times." Officer Chesney sighed and then continued. "I'm so sorry ma'am, but both your daughters were killed instantly. They were pronounced dead at the scene."

Silence.

Dead silence. I couldn't speak. My eyes were fixed on the portrait of my babies, my twin babies, my only babies hanging from the wall. Tori, the oldest, was born at 9:10 A.M., and Dani entered the world four minutes later at 9:14 A.M. My babies were two of the most beautiful children in the entire universe. My twin babies—my fraternal twin babies. As I continued to look at the portrait, I traced their faces with my eyes. Tori was the lighter of the two with a radiant brassy yellow complexion—the color of buttered popcorn. Dani was darker with a dark chocolate skin tone. Both with beautiful big, brown almond-shaped eyes and wide, bright smiles that would melt the heart of anyone who came in contact with them.

I blinked. Tears fell. There was no way in God's name my children were dead. No way.

"Mrs. Prescott. Mrs. Prescott," Officer Chesney said, bringing me out of my daze. "Do you need to sit down?"

"No, I don't." I snapped. "I just need for you to repeat to me what you said because I think you're mistaken. My daughters aren't dead. Just wait. I'll call them right now and prove to you that they are alive and well."

I rushed toward the phone. Before I could pick up the receiver, Officer Kinny, blurted, "Does you daughter Dani have the words PRIMA DONNA tattooed on her right arm?"

I stopped in my tracks. *How'd he know that? I spun around to face the two officers.* "Yeah. Why?"

Officer Kinny walked up and placed his hand on my shoulder. "Mrs. Prescott. I'm so sorry. The paramedics did everything they could to save your daughters, but according to MDOT, they never had a chance, the impact was just too great."

Instantly, I fell to my knees. At once, my heart ached. The mentioning of Tori's keys and Dani's tattoo confirmed my greatest fear—my daughters were dead.

"Noooooooooooooo . . . no, no, no, no," I bellowed. "Not my babies, Lord. Not my daughters. Noooooooooooooo!"

"Janice . . . Janice," I heard someone call. With my hands clutching my chest, I slowly opened my eyes to see my husband, Norman, leaning over me with a fearful look in his eyes.

"Janice, what's wrong? You were screaming and crying in your sleep. You scared me half to death, woman."

I slowly looked around my dimly lit bedroom. I was confused, discombobulated. I looked back at Norman. He was staring at me. "I was asleep?" I whispered.

"Yeah, you were. That must've been some dream you were having 'cause you were screaming, 'No,' tossing, turning, and kicking the comforter off of you."

"Oh, thank you, Jesus," I exclaimed. Thank you, God.

Looking at me as if I were a candidate for the crazy house, Norm said, "What are you thanking Jesus for?"

"'Cause my girls are alive," I shouted.

"Huh?" Norm muttered.

"I had a dream, no a nightmare, that Tori and Dani were killed on I-95. The police showed up at the front door to tell me they'd been killed. It seemed so real."

Norm, with one eyebrow cocked, asked, "Were they together?"

"Yeah. They were in the same car and they were hit by a speeding truck while they were pulled off on the shoulder of the road."

Norm chuckled. "Well, honey, you know that had to be a dream, 'cause Tori and Dani can barely stand to be in the same room together, let alone the same car. One thing we never have to worry about is something happening to them at the same time, while they are together, 'cause they ain't never together."

Norm was right. As much as it broke my heart to admit, my girls had a non-existent relationship. They were as opposite as night and day. They acted more like enemies than sisters—twin sisters at that, and as their mother, it was heart wrenching. I hated that the daughters Norm and I prayed so hard for turned out to be adversaries. It just made me sick.

It took me a minute to collect myself after having such a horrible dream about my children. I'd always feared that something tragic would happen to one of them and the other would be left with insurmountable grief. I also had dreaded thoughts that I'd be six feet under and my girls would be left here on earth still hating each other. I'd been praying for some type of sisterly relationship most of their lives, and years later, nothing has changed. God surely was taking his time with answering this prayer.

Norm had accepted years ago that Tori and Dani would

never have a bond. Although he didn't like it, he had come to live with it. As for me, I just couldn't.

To this day, I often ask God how my girls, who grew in the same womb, shared the same blood type and DNA, also shared the same identical hatred?

I lay my head on the pillow deep in thought. I was still very bothered by the dream and prayed it wasn't some type of sign. "Norm," I softly called.

"Yes, honey," he responded groggily.

"Do you think my dream was a premonition?"

"No, sweetheart. It was just a dream . . . just a dream."

Chapter 1

Tori Faith Prescott
September 2008

A daily exercise regimen was a must. I was not a health fanatic, but I aimed to keep a petite body figure. My workout time also allowed me to relax my mind, clear my head of all negativity and allowed me time to think about the goodness of the Lord.

Usually, I was totally focused while exercising and listening to my favorite gospel tunes. But today, my train of thought was consistently interrupted by my telephone ringing off the hook. The first few times, I ignored it, but it seemed as if the person would hang up and immediately call back. I decided to answer, thinking maybe it was an emergency.

After eyeing the caller ID, I groaned. It was Kyle, my ex-boyfriend. I really didn't want to talk to him, but curiosity got the best of me. "Hello," I answered, in a brusque tone.

"Hey, Tori. It's Kyle. Do you have a minute?" he cheerfully asked, like we were best friends.

"What do you want, Kyle?"

"Sheesh, Tori. Why the attitude?"

"Please. Don't make me go there. You know why I'm not enthused to hear your voice on the other end of my phone."

"Look. I know I messed up. I'm sorry. How many times do I need to say it?"

Rolling my eyes, I responded, "Why are you calling, Kyle?"

"All right. Since you don't seem to want to cut a brotha no slack, I just wanted to call you to tell you that Dani's pregnant."

"What?" I yelled in his ear. "Dani's what?"

"She's pregnant."

I instantly gave him a piece of my mind. "How could you, Kyle? It's bad enough you started dating my sister only months after *we* broke up, then you proposed to her and now she's having your baby? You're disgusting!"

"Tori, I know you hate me. It was wrong for me to get involved with your sister. I admit that. But, it's too late to harp on that now. She's pregnant, and I thought you'd be excited about becoming a new auntie."

"I'm not," I said in a sullen tone.

"Come on, Tori, where's the church girl I once knew? Where's the girl that could forgive and forget like the Bible commands one to do? Where's the girl with the heart of gold?"

"When it comes to Dani, all those qualities are out the window," I spat.

"So, are you coming to the wedding tomorrow? I'd love to see you there."

"Why?"

"I mean, what we had was special. I loved you, Tori. You just didn't want to be with me. Although, I've fallen for your sister, it doesn't take away my love for you."

"And just like I said before, you're disgusting. No, I'm not coming to your wedding, and this conversation is over."

"But Tori—"

I quickly disconnected the call. The nerve of him calling to boast about me becoming an aunt. I couldn't care less. Dani could have ten children, and I'd never have a relationship with any of them because quite frankly, I wouldn't want to have to deal with her and her volatility.

I tried to return to my workout. I couldn't. I was more bothered by Kyle's phone call than I cared to admit. I stopped the fitness DVD and plopped on my sofa. My thoughts were on my past relationship with Kyle. We dated little over two years. I loved him dearly. At the time, I had just started my job as an instructional assistant, working with children with special needs, a job that I enjoyed thoroughly. Initially, my goal was to attend college to become a speech pathologist with the hopes of working with children who displayed difficulties in verbal communication, but college wasn't for me. My heart wasn't in it. So, thirty credits later, I dropped out. I started working as an administrative assistant and promptly realized that job wasn't for me, either. Answering telephones, photo copying and making trips to the mailroom wasn't my cup of tea. My heart was with children. Finally, after searching my brain for a position that was the best fit for me, I applied for and ultimately was offered a job as an instructional assistant, No, I didn't make the money teachers made, but I wasn't in it for money. I was doing what I loved—working with kids.

When Kyle and I began dating, I had just embarked upon my new career. I was twenty-five years old, at the time, and very mature. Kyle, on the other hand, had a lot to learn about being in a relationship. I didn't notice this during the initial stages of our courtship because I was so captivated by his charm and good looks, but I later saw Kyle's true colors.

Kyle and I met on a sunny Saturday morning in Starbucks Coffee. At the register, my mouth craved for my favorite strawberry and crème Frappuccino. I was embarrassed as I reached in my purse to pull out my wallet to pay for my drink, when I noticed I had mistakenly left it at home in the midst of changed purses. Behind me I heard a soft, serene voice say, "I'll pay for it."

When I turned around to face the voice behind me, I melted at the sight of this fine young man standing behind me. I was in awe because of his kindness and his attractiveness.

After purchasing my Frappuccino, Kyle asked if we could sit and chat for a moment. It was the least I could do for the stranger who was so kind to pay for my beverage. Instantly, I was attracted to him. Our conversation flowed as if we had known each other for months. We shared light banter and an abundance of laughter.

Months later, Kyle and I were inseparable. It was what I described as the ideal relationship. We spent morning, noon and night together. We spent time with our families at various gatherings, we attended church services together and Kyle would prepare some of the most romantic picnics in my apartment in the middle of the living room floor. Kyle was definitely on the road to reaching husband status until things gradually began to change. It was if he changed when the season changed.

Once spring and summer-like days approached, Kyle became more consumed with looking good for his stroll to the club scene. Weekly, he made sure his short fade haircut was freshly cut and shaped up. He'd get facials, which he claimed protected the smoothness of his honey brown skin. His nails were always freshly manicured and he made sure he had new gear to show off his muscle bound six-foot body. He had become extremely vain.

Kyle's main focus was night clubs. Every Thursday through Sunday night, Kyle was caught up in the party scene, offering me little to no quality time. It seemed being with the fellas was far more important than spending time with me. This bothered me a great deal. The more time he spent away from me, the more I wondered if there was someone else he was replacing me with. I struggled to keep those negative thoughts out of my mind, but I couldn't shake the feeling that something wasn't quite right with Kyle and his unexplainable actions.

I questioned him about being involved with someone else. He vehemently denied it. I didn't believe him. I told him how uncomfortable I was feeling in our relationship. He promised to change but didn't. I was at my wits end trying to make things like they were between us, but nothing I did made a difference. Then an old conversation I had with my mother popped into my head. I could recall her telling us girls when we were younger, *"If you don't trust him, you don't need to be with him."*

As the summer's end was near, I made one final attempt to reach out to Kyle. I called him and asked if we could spend some quality time together.

He said, "You got that, babe. How about Saturday night?"

I got excited just thinking about it. I was hoping to get things back to the way they were when we first started dating. I was basking in the thought of spending time with my man.

Unfortunately, my hopes were crushed, when he called that Saturday morning to inform me that he had to go out of town with a friend and offered no details when I inquired about the nature of this trip. I was done!

After a two second pause, I huffed, "You know, Kyle, I'm better than this. I am deserving of someone better than you. I don't have to put up with this foolishness any more and I will not! It is over!"

"What?" He said dumbfounded.

"You, me and this so called relationship is over."

"What do you mean, it's over? I love you, Tori."

"Save it, Kyle! You don't know the first thing about loving me. You only love yourself. Your focus is on you and your friends. I can't compete against whatever is it you've got going on in the world and I will not. You are inconsiderate of my feelings and quite frankly I don't trust you."

"Come on, Tori. That's not true. I know I've been partying a lot lately, but best believe it ain't about no other chick. I love you, Tori—only you."

My nostrils were flaring. This Negro was pissing me off. "Look, I have endured this one-sided relationship for months. You're not the same person I met and fell in love with in Starbucks. You've changed and I don't like this new person, therefore, I don't want to do this anymore. It's not healthy for me and now I'm putting me first. Please know that I love you, but it's time for me to let you go."

Kyle chuckled. "Let me go? I'm on my way over so we can talk about this right now."

Sarcastically, I said, "Don't bother. You wouldn't want to leave your *friends* waiting. Besides, when I wanted and needed you, you weren't available. Don't make yourself available to me now. It's a little too late."

"Whatever! I'm on my way."

"Kyle, baby," I spoke softly. "We're done. You'll always hold a special place in my heart. I will always remember the good times we've shared, but as of this moment, there is nothing more to say."

In the midst of Kyle's continued protest, I slowly removed the cordless phone from my ear and pressed the off button. I sobbed at the ending of my romance with Kyle, but ultimately, I had to do what was best for me.

Our relationship ended on a sour note, but it wasn't a nasty separation. I still cared deeply for Kyle even after our break up, however I started to care a little less after I was hit with the news that he was dating my sister. I was hurt-devastated. I vowed that if I ever saw him again, I'd kick him in his groin, although, that has yet to happen.

The phone rang again suspending my thoughts. "Lawd, please don't let this be Kyle again, 'cause I ain't answering." The caller ID displayed my parent's home number. I knew it was probably Mama. "Hey, Mama," I said just after picking up the phone.

"How'd you know it was me?"

"I've got caller ID, remember?"

"Yes, I remember, but it could have been your father."

"You're right, but Daddy doesn't call every day around the same time each evening. That's you," I chuckled.

"Well, baby, you know why I'm calling, right?"

"Nope. I sure don't," I lied. I knew exactly why she was calling, her voice so full of glee.

She asked, "Did you forget about tomorrow?"

Playing the ill-informed role, I asked, "What's tomorrow?"

"It's your sister's wedding. Are you all set to come?"

"Maaaaaa. You know I don't wanna go. Why would you force me to watch my sister marry my ex-boyfriend? That just doesn't make sense."

"'Cause that's your sister, the only sister you've got. If you don't support her, who will?"

"She's never supported me in anything I've done. Besides, she doesn't want me there anyway."

"Yes, she does. You're her sister, and she loves you, believe it or not."

Here we go again. The same old love song my mother sang every time she wanted Dani and me to come together as sisters. I knew my mother hated the relationship between Dani and me, but it was what it was. I tried many times to reach out to Dani with the hopes of forming a sisterly bond, but each time she stuck her nose in the air and said something degrading or belittling to me.

Yes, we were twins, but our similar features were few. I took the dominant genes of my mother who shared the same petite body type and complexion. We both had long, silky hair and full, perky lips. Dani, on the other hand, resembled my father, sharing a darker skin tone. But to me, even with Hershey chocolate skin, she was still pretty. Her hair was short, a tad bit kinky and needed a perm often, but that still didn't diminish her beauty. She was much more beautiful on the outside than she was on the inside.

God knows I'd tried to be a loving, caring sister to Dani, especially after that dreadful accident that happened when we were teenagers.

I will never forget that bright sunny, spring afternoon; I came home elated about our school's upcoming spirit week. Dani didn't participate in many school activities and since spirit week was usually a motivational enhancer for most students. I thought her participation would be like an inspiration "pick me up." I was hoping to get Dani as excited as I was to be involved in the events. I had planned to put our sibling differences aside for a moment to discuss the themes for each day of the school week and possibly collaborate on our outfits.

When I walk into her bedroom, eager to discuss spirit week, I was stunned by what I saw. My sister was passed out in the middle of her floor, appearing lifeless. I called her name. She didn't answer. I slowly walked over to her body and whispered her name. No answer. I noticed an empty prescription drug bottle lying on the floor beside her. My heart started racing. I was scared. I knelt beside her on the floor and placed my hands on her neck to find a pulse. I did, but it was faint. I hurriedly called 911 and then my parents. I thought my sister was going to die.

After a week-long hospital stay and psychiatric evaluations, at age seventeen, Dani was diagnosed with Bipolar Disorder—a mental illness which causes dramatic mood swings. Our family had many sessions with a psychiatrist to learn about this disorder and how to live with someone who suffers from manic to depressive moods swings. It has been the toughest task in my life. There were times when Dani was upbeat and full-of-life and then there were times when trying to get out of bed was as tough as climbing a mountain. She had high and low moments and we never knew what to expect from day to day. During her "normal" days, she and I got along fairly well, but during her moments of depression is when I noticed what appeared to be deep-seeded hatred toward me. I never fully understood why. I brushed it off as her being mentally ill.

My parents were a loving source of support for Dani. They exhibited insurmountable amounts of patience, kindness and understanding. They suffered in silence as they watched Dani go through periods of depression, helplessness, loss of appetite, as well as her manic phase of aggressive behavior, lashing out, and poor judgment. As recommended by the psychiatrist, Dani took medication to decrease the frequency of manic and depressive episodes and participation in psychotherapy—individual and family therapy.

A year after Dani's diagnosis, mom, dad and me participated in a regularly scheduled family session. It was then, I received a shock that send chills down my spine. As research cannot pinpoint, the cause of Bipolar Disorder, Dani had come to her own conclusions. She told the therapist, that I was the cause of her wanting to commit suicide and I was the reason she was suffering from a life-long mental illness. She blamed me. Her statements cut deep. It was at that very moment, our relationship took a turn for the worse. Honestly, I'd never fully forgiven her for blaming me. That was ten years ago and I still carry the hurt I felt that day in my heart.

With proper treatment, people with Bipolar Disorder can still live fulfilling lives. Surprisingly, with her mood instability, Dani was able to obtain two degrees with which she took great pleasure in throwing in my face. She had succeeded in obtaining a bachelor's degree in counseling and a master's degree in school administration. She was now one of the youngest assistant principal's in the Baltimore County Public School's system. For that, she found it necessary to look down upon me because she was so-called educated and getting paid. But for me, it didn't matter. I didn't need money to make me happy. I didn't need a fancy title in front of my name or letters behind my name to complete me. A high-class lifestyle didn't define me. I was secure within myself regardless.

I'd be the first to admit, that feuding with my twin sister was highly immature, especially one with a mental illness but, Dani almost always made the devil come out in me. That's why my objectives for my dear sister was to keep her in prayer and at a distance because she was one witch that could make me lose my religion.

"Ma, I know Dani doesn't want me there, and you know it, too."

"So, are you saying, I'm lying?"

"No, but it's hard for me to believe she wants me there."

"Well, she does, and she told me herself. I know you girls have your ups and downs, but tomorrow is your sister's wedding day, and you need to be there. I know you're grown, Tori, but I'm still your mother and the Bible says, 'Honor thy father and mother and your days on this earth will be longer.' Now, I'm not asking you anymore, I'm telling you to be at that wedding tomorrow at two o'clock."

"But, Ma—"

"Don't 'But Ma' me. Your sister wants you there. Your father and I want you there. So, stop making excuses. You don't want Kyle no more anyway. Aren't you sniffing up under Zachary these days?"

"Yes," I whispered.

"Well, is he enough man to keep you happy?"

I snickered, "Yes."

"There you have it. Let this anger about Dani and Kyle go. Let them go on and be married and raise this new life they've got coming. As long as you gotta man, and he's treating you right, you should have no regrets about letting Kyle go. Now, I'm gonna say this one more time. Dani wants you at her wedding. You need to make it your business to be there."

Sick of hearing her preach to me, I finally agreed to attend. But not before asking her about the baby. "Ma, why didn't you tell me Dani was pregnant?"

"Chile, she told me she was gon' tell you herself. She asked me to keep it a secret so she could break the news to you."

"She didn't tell me anything. Kyle called here a few minutes before you and told me. I just found out today."

"I don't know why they waited so long. Maybe they thought you'd be upset."

"Ummm, yeah," I said sarcastically.

"Well, honey, get yourself prepared for this wedding tomorrow. Welcome Kyle into the family as your brother-in-law, and be ready to greet your new niece or nephew in some months to come. I know it's a hard pill to swallow, Tori, but everything happens for a reason. No, it wasn't right for your sister to go after your ex-boyfriend, but I say forgive and move on. Zachary's a good man, which means you're still a winner in this. Now, what time will I see you at the courthouse tomorrow?"

Courthouse? My sister? Getting married at the courthouse? I was stunned. I couldn't believe my high maintenance sister's wedding ceremony was being held in the chapel of the Mitchell

Courthouse. I was completely awed by my money-making sister planning a courthouse marriage ceremony. Something was up with that. I knew her too well. And every chance she got to spend a dollar to put on a grandiose show, she did.

"I'll see you tomorrow at 2:30?" I teased.

"Tori, don't play with me, girl. You know I said two o'clock. I want to see your face no later then 1:45. A minute after that, you're late."

"Bye, Ma. I'll see you tomorrow," I said just before hanging up. "Damn," I sighed. Then I quickly mouthed, "Excuse me, Lord."

I couldn't believe I had agreed to attend this farce of a wedding. Dani may have fooled my parents and even Kyle, but I shared the same womb with her. I knew her better than anybody. Dani didn't love Kyle. She loved no one more than herself. Self-centered and egotistical were her dominate characteristics. She used Kyle to impregnate her, and I could bet an entire year's salary that although Dani didn't love Kyle, she *did* love the fact that he was stupid enough to fall for her games.

Mentally, I needed to prepare for the ceremony the next day. Watching my sister marry my ex wasn't going to be easy. It was imperative that I sought the Lord aggressively on this because I wasn't so sure that I wouldn't act ugly up in the courthouse.

Chapter 2

Dani Hope Prescott

Sick and nauseated. Those were the feelings that consumed me as I stood at the altar listening to this bootleg minister, who I affectionately named, Reverend Neckbone, perform my wedding ceremony. The fact that I was three months pregnant had nothing to do with my wanting to vomit, but everything to do with that fact that I was marrying a man I didn't love.

"Dani, do you take Kyle to be your lawfully wedded husband, to have and to hold for all the days of your life?" Reverend Neckbone asked.

"I do," I said through almost clenched teeth."

Don't get me wrong. I loved Kyle, but not enough to marry him. I was only standing at the altar because my holy and righteous parents told me that I was not about to bring an illegitimate child into the world. Because of this, I was forced to tie the knot with a man I wasn't in love with.

Poor Kyle. I felt a tad bit sorry for him because he really cared about me. So much so that he was willing to spend his last dime on a big, lavish ceremony. I shut him down immediately. I told him all I wanted was a quick, simple ceremony at the courthouse and a small reception at my parent's house. When he pleaded with me to reconsider, I refused, citing that we needed to save money for the new addition to our family. Since Kyle was a sucker for the baby already, whenever I mentioned not having a big wedding to save money for the little one, he was easily persuaded.

I can't believe I'm doing this, I thought as Kyle recited his vows to me. I looked deeply into his eyes as he softly spoke and saw nothing but genuine love. Too bad I didn't feel the same. Oh, but I got a kick out of seeing my twin sister, Tori, with her face covered with annoyance and resentment because I was marrying her ex-man. That alone was enough to wed a man I didn't really feel undying love for.

I could see Tori's irritated expression out the corner of my eye. I really wanted to turn to her and stick my tongue out, but decided against it. Just knowing her sanctified ass was sitting with her face as tight as a pair of skinny jeans, bearing witness to this marriage was sufficient for me.

I loathed Tori. She was the worst sister ever. My dislike for her started early in life. When we were children, she surrounded herself with snobby friends who treated me as if I were beneath them because my skin was darker. I suffered from a skin condition called Eczema, which causes dry, red, itchy patches on the skin—a condition I developed in childhood. I can recall the times I would be in my room reading a book and they would yell through the crack in my door, "Hey rusty tin skin" or they'd say, "Your skin looks like fish scales." I never responded. I was too proud to let them know they were hurting my feelings, so I would get up and close my door completely shut, and sob.

If anyone knows how cruel children can be, it's me. I also

know that the saying "Sticks and stones may break your bones but words will never hurt you" is a total lie!

As teenagers, Tori quite often teased me about not being attractive enough to get a date. She was right. The Eczema was still a huge issue for me up until age twenty. I didn't attend my ring dance, junior prom or senior prom, and I was never invited to any homecoming dances. But, Tori had guys dropping at her feet. Maybe it wouldn't have been so bad had she not boasted about it. Tori and her friends would walk past me in the hallways at school and enjoyed taunting me. There favorite line to utter in passing was from the movie, *The Color Purple*. Tori said I looked like Celie, so as I traveled to my next class, I'd hear the girls say, "Dani you sho' is ugly." Then they'd laugh as if they told the best joke ever. Sometimes I'd be late to class because I had to stop in the bathroom to wipe the tears from my cheeks.

The ruthless words of my adversaries were nonstop. I never told my parents. I held it all deep within, but it was too painful for any child to endure. The degrading words from a group of haughty females, one being my one and only sister, messed with my self-esteem for years.

Sunday night was the day my mother had chosen to do hair. Each week, she'd alternate which one of us would go first. Every week, Tori somehow managed to take her jabs about the texture of my hair. She'd say my hair was nappy; that Madam C.J. Walker should've been my mother. She was my sister for goodness sake. Why would she put so much energy into mistreating me?

It almost became a daily routine for me to go into my bedroom and hide in the closet and cry until my tears ducts were totally dry. I was depressed a lot, so much so that I finally wanted to give up on life. Although, I was smart, I always felt like I could never live up to the beauty of Tori. I never thought anyone would see me as worthwhile, so I attempted to take my life. That horrible act led to my Bipolar Disorder diagnosis. Yes, they said I was mentally ill, but I didn't believe it. Initially, I fell for the okie doke. But as I grew into adulthood, I realized I was no different than any other person. I had good days and bad days just like everyone else. Everybody gets a little moody at times. Most people have periods of sadness. Everyone acts a little irrational from time to time. In my mind, I was just like every other person on the planet thus my reasoning for not taking my medication or seeing my therapist any longer. What was the use?

Furthermore, the mental illness diagnosis didn't stop me from achieving my goals. Because I had very few friends, I threw myself into my school work. I received a full scholarship to college. I excelled in college and immediately after graduation, I attended graduate school. And the doctors think I'm crazy. No way could I be bipolar with two degrees.

So, now two degrees later, I basked in the joy of rubbing it in Tori's face. Just goes to show that looks aren't everything. And every time an opportunity presented itself for me to repay her for the scars she gave me during my childhood, I gladly jumped at the chance. Hence, me marrying her ex-boyfriend, Kyle.

A few years ago, Miss Thang gave her life to Christ. I guess my parents, who eat, sleep and breathe church, had finally gotten to her. They couldn't to get me. Church and God wasn't my thing. I mean, I believe in God and all, but I refused to sit up in church every Sunday, giving ten percent of my hard earned dollars to some preacher. I wasn't feeling this whole organized religion thing. Besides, I prayed sometimes when I wanted a pay-raise or when the Power Ball jackpot was worth fifty million dollars, but other than that, I couldn't fully get with the church thing.

Now Tori, on the other hand, proclaimed to be serious about the Lord, but she was number one of the list of the church phonies. She had thought of herself as the most beautiful, best-dressed woman in Brice Memorial, but in actuality, she was a stuck up, counterfeit Christian. She wasn't fooling me. She only latched on to that Zachary, the youth minister at Brice, with the hope that he'd soon have his own church, and she'd be first lady. I guess then she could quit her dead-end job and be a stay-at-home wife.

Maybe *I* needed Jesus because the contempt I had for Tori as a child still resided within me at the age of twenty-eight.

My life-long friend Capri said I needed to go back to therapy—that it could possibly help me to deal with Tori, but my response to her was the best way to deal with Tori was through revenge. Marrying Kyle was only the beginning.

Returning my attention back to Reverend Neckbone, he said, "I now pronounce you Mr. and Mrs. Kyle Monroe. Kyle, please kiss your bride."

As Kyle leaned in to kiss me and the applause erupted from the handful of spectators, I immediately knew that I had made a big mistake. I had just entered into a marriage under false pretenses because I wasn't in love with this man, I just wanted his baby. But it sure felt good knowing that I had pierced Tori's heart once I became Mrs. Kyle Monroe.

Chapter 3

Mama

Seven months later—April 2009

"*Dear Lord, our family needs you today more than ever. My baby is suffering dear God and I'm coming to you, to ask you to please strengthen her, Lord. She needs you to get through this tough period in her life, God, and I know as you sit high and look low, with all power in Your hands, you can heal my baby's wombs, God. Wipe her tears away, Lord. Bring peace to her heart, Lord, and Lord maybe this could be a time of healing for my daughters. Maybe this tragedy is what they need to get through this tough time. So, in the precious name of Jesus, I'm asking with a humble heart, to please cover my family, Lord. Heal, deliver and set free. In Jesus' name. Amen.*"

In times such as these, I needed to call on my Lord and Savior 'cause honestly, I didn't know if I was strong enough to help my baby overcome the insurmountable hurt I knew she was feeling. But, I never missed an opportunity to get my girls to bond. So, if I had to use Dani's misfortune to get them together, then so be it.

Again, I prayed, as I dialed Tori's telephone number. I hoped she wasn't still bitter about Dani marrying Kyle. With optimism, I anticipated that her heart would be softened toward her sister once she heard the news. I prayed that my pleas would not fall on deaf ears.

"Hey, Mama. What's up?" Tori answered, cheerfully.

In a soft tone, I said, "Tori, I'm at the hospital with Dani."

"Oh," she nonchalantly said.

"Yes, she went into labor this morning but had some complications during delivery and—"

"And what?"

"The baby was stillborn," I said as tears left my eyes. I could vividly see my new grandson, lying dead in his mother arms.

"Oh, Lord!"

"Tori, your sister is a mess. She can't stop crying, and I think she's quickly fallen into depression. Can you come here to be with her?"

Although Tori sounded genuinely stunned and disheartened by the news, she bluntly responded, "No, Ma. I can't."

"Why not? I just told you your sister's baby died, and you can't come here to be with her?"

"Mama, I'm sorry the baby died. I wouldn't wish that on my worst enemy, but I can't be there for Dani right now. She hasn't spoken to me since the day of her wedding, and even then, it was a snide remark about her being married and I wasn't. I just can't be there for her right now. I'm still dealing with my own issues."

"Tori! Aren't you supposed to be a God-fearing Christian?"

"Don't start with that, Mama. Please don't try to guilt-trip me with the 'aren't you supposed to be a Christian' speech. Like I've said many times before, Dani tests my faith and my walk with God. I know that sounds weak, but the hurt she's caused me is hard to overcome overnight. So, you and everybody else is just gonna have to wait until I'm able to prevail over ill feelings toward her. Right now I'm not. I'm sorry she lost the baby, but as for me coming to her bedside, I just can't do. Not now anyway."

"I'm disappointed in you, Tori. I really am. I can't believe you're acting this way. Dani's your sister for God's sake. Your twin sister."

"Why are you disappointed in me? Just because I won't run to the bedside of the so-called sister who thrives off of making my life miserable? I'm sorry, I'm not gonna do it. At your request, I attended Dani's wedding against my better judgment, and the entire time I felt like I was going to explode. It was only the grace of God that sustained me. But when I walked out of that courthouse, I vowed never to deal with her again."

"For the two of you to be such beautiful girls, you sure do act ugly. Both of you. I'm not gonna dwell on that now. But, you better believe, I'm gonna have a serious talk with both of you real soon because this stuff is getting old. I'm fed up with you so-called sisters. You need to pray about this, Tori because I'm sure God ain't pleased with the hateful words coming out your mouth today."

Tori sat silent on the phone. I didn't know if she was allowing my words to sink in her thick skull or if she was quiet to show her disinterest in my phone call. After several seconds of silence, I decided to give up on convincing her to come to the hospital.

"You know what, Tori? Do as you see fit. I'm going back in the room with your grieving sister. Talk to you later." I hung up.

I wasn't lying when I said I was disappointed in Tori. I've

always expected more from her because she was my meek, mild child. She was the friendly one, the forgiving one. She was the one who put Christ in the center of her life. So, I expected her to be more willing to put her differences with her sister aside knowing that she experienced a traumatic event.

I stood in the hospital waiting room with my head rested against the wall. As I massaged my temples, I thought back to the day Norm and I found out I was pregnant with twins. We were so excited. Norm picked up lots of literature about twin births. I recalled reading that twins were born with an automatic, special bond just because they shared the same womb. From the moment both fertilized eggs were implanted into the uterine wall at the same time, a connection should have formed. At least that's what Norman and I expected when we learned I was in fact pregnant with twins after two years of trying to conceive a baby with no success.

During the pregnancy, we had envisioned what we thought their lives would be like. We foresaw their closeness—being best friends, being joined at the hip, dressing alike, shar-ing their own language, having the same interests and participating in the same activities. We were excited about their impeding arrival and couldn't wait to share them with the world.

Norm and I were proud parents. There was no doubt in our minds that Tori and Dani weren't perfect children. But it didn't take long for us to realize the relationship between our daughters was nothing like we had imagined. The bond we expected seemed absent. In hindsight, I realized that what I thought were Braxton Hicks contractions were really Tori and Dani fighting in the womb.

As infants, they fought over bottles and pacifiers. As toddlers they fought over stuffed animals. As pre-schoolers they clashed over Legos and those wooden ABC/123 blocks. During the grade school years they argued over coloring books and crayons. The middle school years only brought on more bickering and physical altercations over the television they shared and who Mommy and Daddy loved best. This was also the era when they decided they wanted separate friends and didn't want to attend the same parties or outings with each other.

In high school, Tori and Dani's dislike for each other escalated. They began to lash out verbally and say mean and hurtful things. No day passed that Norman and I didn't hear, "I hate you" or "I wish you were dead" or "I wish you weren't my sister." They fought over clothes. They quarreled over boys, who was smarter, who was prettier, who was more popular and an infinite list of superficial quarreling that made Norm and I sick to our stomachs.

Many nights, we'd wondered what happened. These were the babies we prayed for. These girls were our little miracles. So, why in the world did God bless me with two children who had such disdain for each other?

Chapter 4

Tori

"Tori, what's wrong? You look upset," Zachary asked, rushing toward me after hearing me slam the cordless phone on the base. "Who was that on the phone?"

Angrily I responded, "My mother."

"What'd she say that's gotten you so upset?"

"She called to tell me Dani's baby died. It was a boy. He was stillborn."

"Oh, Lord," Zach said, disheartened. "What happened?"

I shrugged. "I don't know all the details. All I know is that the baby died."

"Well, let's get you over to the hospital. You should be with your family now."

Zach didn't give me a chance to respond before he started running around my apartment looking for his keys to drive me to a place I had no intentions on going.

"Zach . . . stop," I yapped.

He turned around to look at me with a stunned expression on his face. He wasn't used to me speaking to him in this manner. "What do you mean stop? Don't you wanna go?"

"Nope."

"What do you mean, no?" His face was now covered with a confused frown.

"Just like I said. I'm not going?"

"And why not?"

"Because I have nothing to say to my sister right now. I'm sorry she's hurting but, there is nothing I can do for her."

"Tori Prescott," he snapped. "I cannot believe I just heard those words come out your mouth. This *is* your sister we're talking about, right?"

I knew the moment he said my full name, a lecture slash counseling session was about to occur because it's embedded in his soul to provide guidance. In fact, that's how we met. Zachary was the eighth grade counselor at Lake Brooke Middle school when I first joined the staff there as an instructional assistant. On the staff's first day back to school, we met in the library for a staff meeting and the Welcome Back Breakfast. It was during that meeting each staff member introduced themselves. When he stood up to speak and introduced himself as Zachary Ambrose, the eighth grade guidance counselor, I was immediately attracted to him because he resembled my favorite actor Will Smith. When he spoke, his words had an eloquent and instant flow. I felt something tingling in my spirit.

A few weeks after the start of the school year, Zach would find his way to my classroom to engage in small talk. Not about anything serious. He just wanted to chat. But, I noticed then he was feeling me. He didn't verbally announce it until months later. It was a few days before Thanksgiving break when he asked me out for lunch. That was the beginning of our budding romance. It didn't take me long to fall in love with Zach. He was always the perfect gentlemen, and because he was spiritually grounded, that made the relationship even better. He respected my position on pre-marital sex—that I was not engaging in it. No, I wasn't a virgin, but I made a vow to God that I wouldn't sleep with another man, after my break-up with Kyle, unless he was my husband.

A few months after Dani married Kyle, Zach proposed to me. The proposal came as I shock, but I was elated to say yes. Soon after the proposal, we set a date for July 2009. I loved this man, for I felt he was my soul mate. Not only was he handsome, tall and debonair, but he was also educated. He had earned a master's degree in counseling from Howard University and had hopes to obtain a doctoral degree in theology.

Shortly after we began dating, he became a member of Brice Memorial and immediately Pastor Brice took Zach under his wing. Just recently, he had been appointed the new Youth Minister. With this new position, Zach felt he needed more education thus his desire to obtain a doctorate degree.

Now, as much as I loved this man, I wasn't in the mood for one of his lectures. I wasn't one of his at-risk youth he worked with at the school or church. I was his fiancée, and I needed a light bulb to go off in his head to make him realize that I wasn't budging on this issue with Dani. I had made up my mind and nobody was going to change it. Nobody.

"Yep, she's my so-called sister, but I can't deal with her right now."

"Why? You still mad that she married your ex-boyfriend?" I looked at him with contempt. How dare he throw that in my face? He continued. "You know, I slightly understood you being upset at that time, but that was seven months ago. If you're still mad about it today, then you're more hung up on this guy than you let on. So, if your reason for not wanting to go see your sister in her time of need is because you're still mad that she married, Kyle, then you and I need to have a serious talk. I love you, Tori, but I ain't about to marry you if you're still hung up on some other guy."

I was furious. "Zachary," I screamed. "How could you of all people say that to me? You know my issues with Dani go way beyond her marrying Kyle. She's often treated me like dirt, and you know this. My ill feelings toward her didn't just start today or seven months ago. So, don't tell me that this is about her and Kyle 'cause it's not."

In a much softer tone, he said, "Tori, I'm sorry. I shouldn't have said those things to you. But, you know what the Bible says about forgiveness. I can't understand why you don't apply all your biblical knowledge to this mess with your sister."

"I'm gonna repeat to you—once again—my scars with Dani are deep. And all biblical principles go out the window when it comes to her."

"So, you're only a Christian when you're not dealing with your sister?"

"You got it," I smugly said. I knew that would tick him off, but I didn't care. That was how I felt.

"I'm disappointed in you, Tori. You know better."

"Join the club. Mama's disappointed in me, too. Maybe you all can create a "Disappointed in Tori Club" and give out free membership passes to anyone else who wants to unite with y'all."

Grabbing his keys, he said, "I can't talk to you when you're like this. There's no getting through to you. Maybe I'll go to the hospital myself to offer my condolences since you won't. Then I'm going home."

"Then by all means, do what you have to, Minister."

Zach looked at me with disgust. His look stung. Without saying another word, he shook his head and walked out the door. No goodbye—no nothing.

My heart was immediately filled with sadness. Tears began to roll down my face. I needed to pray. But before I dropped to my knees to talk to God, I couldn't help but wonder why Zach cared so much. My relationship with Dani shouldn't have affected him one way or another, so why was he concerned?

Chapter 5

Dani

I wasn't in the mood to have Kyle, Mommy and Daddy hovering over me upon my return from the hospital. I just wanted to grieve alone. I recognized that they were deathly afraid that I might've fallen into one of my Bipolar depression episodes and were just concerned about my well being, but honestly I didn't want it. They didn't understand my pain. None of them had ever lost a child.

"Hey, honey," Kyle spoke tenderly as he entered the bedroom interrupting my thoughts.

"Hey," I coldly responded.

Ignoring my attitude, he asked, "Do you want me to bring you up something to eat? Your mother just brought over some of her homemade chicken noodle soup. It looks great."

"No, Kyle. I just want to be alone."

"Baby, I don't want you to go through this alone. I'm grieving too. We need each other to get through this."

Weeping, I uttered, "I know you're hurting too, Kyle, but you can't begin to imagine how I feel. I walked in the hospital pregnant, prepared to give birth to our son. Instead I left with an empty womb, no baby and a broken heart.

Kyle was now holding my hand. He gently kissed my forehead. "Dani, we can get through this. The worse thing you could do is isolate yourself right now. You need the support of your family."

"I know, but I feel like there is nothing anyone can say to or do to make it better. I've never felt pain like this before."

"That's exactly why you need us by your side. There needs to be a balance between grieving alone and sharing the grief. Don't carry this on your shoulders without help. We're all in this together."

I was becoming a bit frustrated with Kyle. I understood fully what he was trying to do, but he needed to understand that nothing or no one could cure my grief. Instead of going back and forth with him, I calmly said, "I'll think about what you said, but for now I'd just like to be alone. I hope you don't mind."

"No problem, sweetie. I understand. Just holler if you need anything. I'll be downstairs chatting with your parents."

"Close the door behind you."

Kyle left without saying a word. I was elated that he had chosen to keep my parents entertained downstairs so they wouldn't come up to my bedroom to bother me. I just wanted to stare at the salmon colored walls in peace. I didn't need my holy-rolling parents offering their prayers or Godly advice because I wasn't up for it. Especially since God allowed my baby to die. If there was truly a God in heaven, He wouldn't allow bad things to happen to good people, especially babies.

Every time I thought about those innocent people who died in the World Trade Center, The Pentagon and in Pennsylvania on September 11, 2001, I wondered where

God was. The thought of the Asian Tsunami, responsible for over 200,000 people losing their lives and having their land inundated by an insurmountable amount of water disgusted me. Where was God then? And don't get me started on how all those people suffered in New Orleans during and after Hurricane Katrina. Where was omnipresent God on that particular day in August 2005? I just couldn't find it within myself to get caught up into this whole religion thing because God always seemed to disappoint me.

Despite my current feelings, I was raised in a Christian home. There was no living in the home of Janice and Norman Prescott and not attending church. And not only did we attend church, we had to be active in ministry. Tori and I sang in the children's choir, served on the junior usher board and the dance ministry. Growing up in the home of two God-fearing Christians, there was no way I could escape going to the house of the Lord. But, once I left home to attend college at Hampton University, my views began to change. I started to question God a lot—starting with the hellish relationship I had with my twin sister, Tori. But, after enduring all her taunts about my skin color and the Eczema, and especially her being the cause of my failed suicide attempt, I gave into her evil ways thus our relationship today. What she never banked on was that I'd be the overachiever with two degrees and a highly respected career as an assistant principal with flawless skin. Because of improved medical treatments, there were no signs that I ever suffered from a skin condition. And even with a so-called disability, I was a respected and productive member of society.

Some would say, my success should be all the revenge

I needed against Tori, but my bruised heart said it wasn't enough.

I also had serious doubts about my relationship with God during my freshman year away at school, my Pop Pop, my father's father, passed away from cancer. He was my rock, and he embraced me—dark-complexion, dry, red, itchy skin, nappy hair and all. Besides, I favored my father more which in turn made my relationship with my paternal side of the family much stronger than those of my mother's side of the family.

My junior year at college brought about more death when my Grandma Rosena, my mother's mother died from heart failure. I was grief stricken and had to suffer through the death of my grandmother all alone in my dorm room. My family didn't come to get me, but they did send money via Western Union for a bus ticket to make it home for the funeral. Once again, I began questioning God and wondered if there was even a Heavenly Father.

I'd gone through a number of trials and tribulations in my twenty-eight years, most recently the death of my baby, which was consequently my reason for not attending church any longer. Out of respect for my parents, I did attend on special occasions, but I'd never planned to be a faithful, bible-toting Christian like Tori. This disappointed my parents, but so be it. I was grown.

Curled up under my Down comforter, I sighed when I heard a knock at the door. My initial thought was to ignore it, to act as if I was asleep, but I decided against it. "Who is it?" I snapped.

"It's Mama. Can I come in?"

Wanting badly to say 'no', I didn't. After all, she was my

mother and had been by my side since the day I was rushed to the hospital enduring those dreadful contractions.

"Yeah, Ma. Come in."

She peeked her head through the door and asked, "Were you sleeping?"

"No. I was just lying here—thinking."

Entering the room, she walked over to sit down at my bedside. "Dani, I'd be lying if I said I know how you feel because I don't. But, I do sympathize with you and will be praying for you to heal from this unfortunate event."

"Thanks, Ma. I appreciate it." It was a true statement. I wasn't totally against prayer or God, I just doubted Him.

"Have you decided what you are going to do about work?"

"Yes. It's May—almost the end of the school year. So, I'm considering not going back until after the school year ends. Kyle already talked to Shelley—the Principal at my school, and she told him to tell me to take as much time as I needed. Besides, I was going to be on maternity leave for most of the summer anyway, so I may just turn it into bereavement leave."

"Well, baby, you've got to do what's best for you. Norm and I were talking last night and wondered if you'd consider going back to counseling—maybe at the church with Pastor Brice could be a start if you don't want to go back to psychotherapy."

Rolling my eyes, I said, "No disrespect, Ma, but I don't want to talk to nobody at the church. I don't want those people in my business, including Pastor Brice. He's way too close to Zach. I don't want Zach and Tori in my business."

"Dani, don't start. This conversation has nothing to do with Tori or Zach. It's about you finding some support to help you heal from this tragedy."

"I'll think about it, Ma. I'll go on the Internet in a little bit to find a new therapist since Dr. Shapiro, my former doctor has now retired."

"You promise?" Mama asked with a slight smile.

"I promise," I returned her smile.

"OK. Well, me and your daddy are going to get on home. He's praying for you, too. We'll call to check on you tomorrow."

Reaching my arms out to hug Mama, I said, "I love you."

"I love you, too. Now, go get on that computer and find a new counselor. Oh, and don't forget that the church's anniversary is in two weeks. I want you and Kyle in church on that day."

I didn't respond. I just smiled and watched her leave the room. I looked over toward my oak wood dresser and eyed my laptop. I crawled out of bed, and slowly walked over to my dresser to retrieve it.

Once I got back into bed, it was my intention to stay true to the promise I made to my mother and look into counseling, but instead I logged on to my Yahoo! e-mail account. There were fifteen unread messages in my inbox. I scrolled up and down my inbox only to see a bunch of forwarded messages from my friend, Capri. I absolutely adored my friend, Capri Patterson. She possessed beauty on the inside and out. Her glowing smile and gentle features reminded me of actress, Sanaa Lathan. Inside, she had a heart of gold. *She* was truly my sister.

There were a few messages from college acquaintances and colleagues. Most of the stuff I rarely read. But, one subject in my inbox caught my attention: WISH I WAS THERE. I smiled. I clicked on the subject to read the entire message:

***

Hey Sweetness,

I'm so sorry for your loss. You know if I could be there for you, I would. If there is anything I can do for you, please don't hesitate to ask. When you get a free moment, call my cell phone. Stay strong, sweetness. Just hold on until we see each other again. I'll be sure to stroke your wombs.

One Love,

Me

Receiving that message was all the comfort and counseling I needed. There was no need for me to do an Internet search for counseling because that email was all the therapy I desired to assist me with getting back on track.

I started to dial that pre-paid, secret cell phone number after I read the email, but with Kyle lurking around, I didn't want to chance it. But just a message to know that I was on his mind made me content.

For the first time since my son's death, I smiled. I closed my laptop, placed it on the floor beside my bed, laid my head on my soft, cushioned pillow and drifted into a peaceful sleep.

Chapter 6

Tori

Early Sunday morning, my telephone rang before I even had a chance to sip on my hot cup of coffee. "Hey, baby." It was Zach. We hadn't said more than five words to each other since the disagreement we had about Dani. I avoided him at work, and most times, I evaded his phone calls. Since it was the Lord's day, I decided to take his call.

"Oh, hey," I said unenthused. I was still pissed about his comments about Kyle. I needed him to apologize before I could move on.

"I just wanted to know if you wanted me to pick you up for church this morning."

"Nope."

"Come on, Tori. Are you still mad over our little tiff? It's been almost two weeks now. It wasn't really that serious."

"Well, it was to me. You accused me of still being hung up on Kyle, and that's not true."

"OK, Tori. I'm sorry. It was wrong of me to say the things I did that night. I've tried to apologize before now, but you always seemed too busy to speak to me or weren't taking my calls. I think we were both a little heated that night and said some things we didn't mean. Again, I'm sorry for that. Now, can you please forgive me?"

I sat quietly on the phone. I didn't respond right away.

"Pweeeeeeeeeease", he said in a baby voice.

I laughed. He knew I couldn't stay mad at him forever. I just needed an apology. "Thank you, Zach. I accept your apology. I'm sorry, too, for being so mean that night."

"Good," he said with a sigh of relief. "Now, I'm on my way to pick you up. Be ready. I don't wanna hear, 'I still need to put my make-up on' or 'I just ran my panty-hose and I need to change them.' Be ready. It's anniversary Sunday at the church, and I want to be on time. Got it?"

"Bye, Zach. I'll be ready."

I smiled. I was glad we were able to resolve our differences. An apology went a long way. I was glad he was man enough to realize his mistakes.

My phone rang just as I was about to apply my make-up. "Hello?"

"Praise the Lord, Tori. How are you on this blessed day?"

"I'm fine, Mama. How are you?"

"Chile, I'm wonderful. I was calling to check on you, to make sure you were getting ready for church."

"I am. Zach will be here to pick me up shortly, and you know how he gets when I'm running late."

"Well, I'll let you go then. I'll see you in service."

"OK, Mama. Love you."

My Mama. Janice Prescott. Some would say she was more my twin than Dani because we looked so much alike with matching complexions, size twelve frames, and long, silky hair.

At fifty-five years old, Mama exemplified dignity and

elegance, but if need be, she could give you a good tongue lashing—kind of like Judge Mabeline Ephrine from Divorce Court. She could tell you off, all in the name of love. She also could be a bit overbearing, bossy and controlling. But, I still loved her. I just knew how to tune her out when necessary.

Mama enjoyed her career as an events coordinator. She loved planning events, and she was good at it. She was very creative, detailed-oriented and a good planner. Before Dani and I were born, Mama worked at the Student Activities center at Coppin State University. But toward the end of her pregnancy, she stopped working. Raising twins was no easy feat, especially feuding twins. So, from the time Mama was put on bed rest until we entered high school, she didn't work. It wasn't until after she felt we didn't need her as much anymore that she desired to reenter the working world. And surprisingly enough, after so many years of being away, Coppin State welcomed her back with open arms.

She also planned most of the events at the church. Pastor Brice loved her input, and she loved giving it. So, for every Brice Memorial, bridal shower, baby shower, wedding, birthday party or whatever the occasion, Events Coordinator Janice Prescott had her hands in it.

As promised, I was all set to go when Zach pulled in front of my apartment building. "Good morning," I said as I entered the car. I leaned over and kissed him gently on the cheek.

"Wow. You look beautiful. The color fuchsia complements your gorgeous skin."

I smiled. I was glad he noticed. I had bought a new pleated skirt suit for the church's anniversary. It was stylish, and its beautiful spring color went well with the sunny April weather.

I already knew I looked good, but Zach's comments instantly made my head swell.

It didn't take long for us to arrive at the church because I only lived about ten minutes away. Besides, Zach drove like a NASCAR driver, so it probably took us no more than five. We parted ways once we entered the church, so he could meet with Pastor Brice in his study before service began. I entered into the sanctuary then headed toward my usual pew where I sat with my parents.

"Hi, Daddy."

"Good morning, Tori," he said. "How are you?"

"I'm fine, Daddy. Where's Mama? She called me this morning to make sure I was up and ready for church."

Daddy chuckled. "I hope you've figured out that no matter how old you girls get, your mother is always going to treat you like her babies."

"I know, Daddy." Then I leaned over to him and whispered, "I'm glad you don't treat us like that." He snickered.

It was true. Norman Prescott was a wonderful father. His support of Dani and me was unwavering. Although, he hated the bickering and the cat fights, he never took sides, and he rarely intervened unlike Mama. Honestly, I think after so many years of enduring the madness, he just became immune to it all. Nevertheless, he never judged or criticized, but he didn't hesitate to tell us to be quiet if he was just sick and tired of hearing the noise.

As a retired, Baltimore County Police Officer, Daddy now worked part-time as a Drug Abuse Resistance Education (DARE) instructor in various schools throughout Baltimore County. We wondered why after thirty of years on the police force, he wouldn't just sit home and enjoy his retirement, but he said he was too young to be sitting at home. However, he did make time for his favorite leisure activities such as playing golf, watching sports and men's fellowship functions at the church.

He was fifty-seven years old and was a good looking older gentlemen. People often told him he looked a lot like T.D. Jakes, but a much thinner version. He also wasn't as thunderous as the famed preacher. Daddy was a mild-mannered man, but like Jakes, he was a praying man. He loved the Lord and growing up, there wasn't a day he didn't speak on His goodness and mercy.

Daddy never takes credit for any of his accomplishments, such as having a house built in 1979 from the ground up with little or no money. He and Mama didn't have the money they had now, but Daddy always proclaimed that it was the grace of God that allowed him to build a home for his family. He didn't have a college degree, but had advanced to the position of lieutenant before he retired. He says it was nothing but the goodness of the Lord. He never took credit for the blessings in his life, he gave all honor to God. But I often wondered if he questioned God about the relationship between his daughters. I'd planned to visit that subject one day.

"Daddy, who is the—"

"Hi, Daddy," an unpleasant familiar voice sang just as I was about to continue my conversation with my father. I knew who the voice belonged to, but I had to force myself to look— to confirm the identity of person behind the voice— because I was in church and it wasn't one I usually heard in the house of worship.

I looked up just as my father stood to hug Dani, who

looked like she was dressed to go out to a night club rather than church. Her black and white halter top dress revealed more cleavage than necessary and was hugging her hips.

"Hey, Dani," Daddy said. "It's good to see you in the house of the Lord. I thought Janice was kidding when she said you were coming today. Where's Kyle?"

"Now, Daddy. You know I always come on special occasions," she bragged as if that was something to be proud of. "Kyle is on his way in. He's parking the car."

When Dani looked over at me, I quickly turned away. I wasn't about to part my lips to say a word to her. She had actually just ruined my entire Sunday by showing her face in Brice Memorial.

The atmosphere immediately changed upon her arrival. I didn't feel like I was in a place of worship anymore, but more so in a dirty, abandoned warehouse. That was the kind of environment she created when she entered a room. To make matters worse, Mama walked up and was happy as a kid in a candy store when she saw "her girls" in church.

"Hey, my babies," Mama said, smiling. "I'm glad to see y'all here and on time. It's gonna be a lovely anniversary service." Then she whispered, "I know 'cause I coordinated it again this year."

Mama was interrupted when Larry Johnson, the very married Larry Johnson, walked up grinning from ear to ear, breaking his neck to speak to Dani. Larry and Dani go way back. They had been an item a few years back, but as Dani always does, she treated him like crap. He eventually moved on, got married and has an infant daughter. But, for whatever reason, he seemed to still be stuck on Dani, drool falling from his lips every time he saw her.

I watched as Dani flirted with this man as if she wasn't standing in the sanctuary. I eyed them both with disgust. She gently placed her hand on his face and mouthed seductively, "It's so good to see you, L.J. My you're looking quite fine today." *Did this whore have any shame in her game?* The only reason he looked fine to her was because he was married. If he was free and single, she'd want no parts of him. Sadly, she is drawn to the man in a committed relationship with a girlfriend, fiancée or wife. Go figure.

Just as the praise and worship team assembled in the pulpit, Mama said, "Come on, girls. We're all sitting together today. Make sure you save room for Kyle."

I thought I'd die. I wasn't about to share my favorite pew with the devil. So, I politely excused myself and said I had to go to the bathroom with no plans to return to my familiar seat. Before I could get out of the pew into the aisle, Mama said, "Don't forget Sunday dinner at the house after church. We do this every year. This year is no different, so I don't want excuses."

I just shook my head and walked away. My mother always created a reason for a family Sunday dinner, and when she planned a dinner there was no getting out of it unless you were hospitalized, incarcerated or dead. Other than that you had to attend.

Brice Memorial's 100th church anniversary was turning out to be the worse. Not only did I have to be in the company of Dani and Kyle, but I had to break bread with them after church. Lord, how was I gonna make it through this day without losing my religion or my mind?

Chapter 7

Dani

Just as I was about to take my seat in the pew, my eyes landed upon one of the loves of my life, Brendan Hall. My thoughts immediately went into the gutter, as this Kobe Bryant look-alike, headed in my direction. "Hi Brendan," I said as we embraced. I closed my eyes to take in his scent. He always smelled so delicious.

"Hello to you, Miss Lady. My goodness, I wanna eat you up right here, you're looking so good."

I chuckled, "Boy stop. You know church ain't the place for that." Brendan was a former colleague before I became assistant principal. Although not officially in a relationship, Brendan and I were "friends with benefits." The most beneficial part of our friendship was when I'd call and he'd be readily available to provide maintenance when I needed to be serviced.

The chemistry between us was ever present. I kind of felt others were staring at us, so I attempted to downplay our conversation especially since Kyle would be coming in soon.

"I see your hubby coming, Kyle spoke. I'll holla at you later." He whispered. I smiled and waved Kyle over to where we were sitting. He looked at me suspiciously and said, "I see Brendan ran away in a hurry."

"He didn't run, Kyle. He's getting ready for service."

"Yeah, right. Just make sure you keep ole boy out your face." His tone was firm, but I didn't care.

"Whatever, Kyle." Kyle was jealous of any male who showed me any attention. Sadly, with Brendan, he might've been right. Any man who could lay it down in the bedroom like Brendan would always have his number on speed dial.

The church anniversary service wasn't too bad. The singing, the sermon, the entire atmosphere was not as dreadful as anticipated. However, my mother inviting Kyle and me for Sunday dinner was bound to be dreadful. Oh, how I wanted to say no, because the last thing I wanted was to see Tori acting all lovey dovey with her fiancé. I was sure the sight of them was going to make me sick. I started to play the depressed, mournful card so I could skip dinner, but I decided against it because I knew my mother looked forward to this Sunday dinner every year. Had it not been for her, I would have most certainly taken my ass home.

After church ended, Kyle and I made our way to the car and headed toward my parents home. As we approached the front door of the ranch-style single family home, Kyle grabbed my hand. "You up for this?" he asked.

"Kyle, I'm cool. I ain't thinking about Tori today."

"That's good to hear. We're just gonna have a pleasant dinner and go home. No fussing, no arguing, no nothing," he said, basically giving me the rules of this engagement. "Then once we get home, maybe we can have dessert." He gently nibbled my ear.

I was so glad he couldn't see my face because my eyes had rolled all the way to the back of my head. The last thing I wanted was to have *dessert* with Kyle. Actually, I was hoping to have an email waiting for me so I could go have dessert somewhere else.

Daddy must have heard Kyle and me talking at the front door, because he opened it with a huge grin. "Dani, Kyle, come on in here. We were waiting for y'all. Your mother just put some hot, buttered rolls on the table."

"Sounds good, Mr. Prescott," Kyle told him. "My stomach was growling the entire service, so hot rolls sound good to me."

When Kyle and I entered the house, I walked straight into the living room to put my purse on the sofa. Kyle had gone directly into the dinning room, but I wanted to take my time. Was I really ready for a sit-down family dinner with Tori? I knew we had a horrible relationship, but Miss Sanctified Christian didn't have the decency to send her condolences through our parents or anything. It stung for a moment. In my mind, it still wasn't right and truth be told, I was pissed about it. Now, I was being forced to have dinner with this wench.

"Hey, everybody," I said as pleasantly as I could. "I hope I didn't keep you hungry too long." I was trying to be nice, but I could feel Tori's stares. In an effort to keep the peace, I didn't even look her way.

"Sit on down at this table, girl. We were just about to bless the food," Mama instructed.

I quickly sat down next to Kyle. Tori and Zach were seated directly across from us, and my parents were at opposite ends of the table. My father being the head of the household was at the head of the table ready to say grace.

"Let's us pray. Dear Lord, make us truly thankful for which we are about to receive for the nourishment of our bodies. In Jesus name we pray. Amen."

"Amen," we all said in unison.

Immediately, Daddy and Kyle started piling food on their plates. No one spoke. You could feel the tension in the room. The tension between Tori and me. The tension between Tori and Kyle. The tension between Kyle and Zach. It was tension all over the place. I just hoped there wouldn't be any blood shed in Mama's beautifully black and white dining room suite. I was pretty sure she'd have a serious fit if we came remotely close to messing up her white cloth dining chairs or the white porcelain china closet that housed her antique tableware.

Tori was the first to break the silence. "Mama, where in the world did you find time to fix all this food? Weren't you in church all day?"

"I cooked the collard greens and potato salad last night. Early this morning, I put the ham and the macaroni and cheese in the oven. And as soon as I rushed through the door after church, I put on a pan of fried chicken and dropped the catfish in the deep fryer."

Mama had always been a good cook. Her Sunday meals always looked like the Sunday dinners from the movie *Soul Food*. Once we were grown and out of the house, she didn't cook as much food, but when she knew we were coming over, we knew to expect a soul food feast.

"Ummmm, Mrs. Prescott, this catfish is delicious," Kyle said with a mouth full of food.

"Thank you, Kyle. And when are you gonna stop calling me Mrs. Prescott? You've been my son-in-law for eight months now. Call me Mama."

Kyle chuckled. And with collard green juice running down the side of his mouth, he said, "Will do, Mama. Will do."

"And speaking of sons-in-law," Daddy spoke. "How's the wedding planning going for you, Tori? I haven't heard much about it lately."

"Things are going well, Daddy," she answered. "Mama didn't tell you I picked out my dress?"

"No, she didn't."

Mama interjected. "Yes, I did, Norm. You just wasn't listening to me. It was the same day we had come back from looking at Martin's West Banquet Hall for the reception. Remember when I told you the facility had a bridal room and Tori could get dressed there?"

"I think," Daddy said, looking confused.

I was sure Mama had told him all about it, but just like most men, he couldn't care less about a wedding.

Mama continued. "Anyway, that was the day Tori and I bought her dress."

"Well, congrats to you, Tori. I'm sure the dress is beautiful," Kyle said.

"I hope it ain't all white," I mumbled under my breath.

"As a matter-of-fact, it is all white," Tori responded to my not so subtle comment. "Do you have a problem with that?" She was full of attitude.

Trying to remain tactful, I replied, "Nope. Not at all."

Attempting to intervene on a possible argument, Kyle said, "Zach, have you gotten your tuxedo, yet?"

"Not yet. I need to go to AfterHours Tuxedo for a fitting real soon though or Tori's going to have my hide."

Mama and Daddy chuckled.

"Take it from me, Zach. There ain't no rush," Daddy said. "This wedding is for the women. Getting your tuxedo is the simple part. So, I'm sure you've got time."

"Daddy," Tori huffed.

"Please don't put that in his head. He's already procras-tinating as it is. If you tell him there's no rush, he may not go until the week before the wedding."

"I won't, sweetheart. I promise. I'll go this week," Zach reassuringly told Tori.

The conversation was making me ill. It went from the tuxedo to the bridesmaids dresses, to the ceremony and reception music to the flowers. I had had enough wedding talk to last me the rest of the year. It was this conversation that sent me straight into bitch mode.

"Soooooooooooo, Zach," I called, pointing my fork at him while twirling it in the air. "Are you sure you ready for this marriage thing? It's a lot of work, ya know. Almost like another fulltime job."

He looked at me strangely before he answered, "Yes, I'm sure. I know it's a big step, but I love Tori. I know marriage can be a challenge, but I'm up for it. Besides, God is on our side. With Him, we'll be able to handle any and everything that comes our way."

Oh, yeah, I thought. "So, then you're up for not having children? I know most men want children and Tori can't have any."

"Dani," Tori snapped.

I heard the silverware fall on my father's plate. I heard my mother gasp. It was about to be on.

"What?" I snapped back at her.

"Dani, what do you mean, I won't be having children?" Zach asked, looking dumbfounded.

Staring at Tori, I said, "Oh, you didn't tell him?"

"Tell me what?" Zach questioned.

"Dani, stop," Daddy pleaded.

Sarcastically I said, "She's just like Sarah in the Bible. She's barren. She can't have children."

"You witch," Tori yelled. "How could you?"

I sat back in my chair with a smug look on my face. "It ain't my fault you didn't tell him. If he's gonna be your husband, shouldn't he know his future wife can't have kids?"

"It wasn't your place to tell him, Dani," Mama hissed. "There was no reason to even bring that up at this dinner table. You said that with the intention to create drama."

"No, I didn't, Mama. How was I supposed to know she didn't tell Zach she is unfruitful? He was all boasting about how they could handle any and everything that came their way, so I wanted to know if he was up for not being a father. I think it was a reasonable question."

"No, it wasn't," Tori screamed. "You did it to be a smart. That's how arrogant, pompous, small-minded folks like you do. You make me sick, Dani. You better be glad I respect our parents' house 'cause if I didn't, I'd reach over this table and smack your lips in the back of your head." The look in Tori's eyes was one of fury. I had really gotten her goat.

I snickered. "Come on, big sister, Tori. Come smack me. I dare you."

Tori didn't speak another word. She jumped from her chair, throwing her cloth napkin into her plate then charged toward me. I quickly stood, preparing myself to do battle.

"Tori, stop it," Daddy yelled. Zach grabbed Tori and stopped her just before she reached my side of the table. He held her tightly as she struggled violently to get away from him.

Daddy stood, and he was ticked. "You're not gonna fight your sister, Tori. You're too old to be acting like this. And on the Lord's day at that." Then he turned to me and bellowed, "You, too, Dani. Why can't we have one, just one peaceful gathering without you saying something out your mouth to hurt your sister? Is it that hard to do? This mess with y'all is getting old . . . hell, it's been old, and I refuse to allow the two of you with your ugly ways to stop me from enjoying a meal with my family. Now, either we sit down and break bread together in love, or y'all have to go—both of y'all. Now which one is it?"

Wow. I was shocked. Daddy was basically inviting us to leave. This was a first. I didn't even know how to respond. I didn't want to continue to eat dinner with Tori, but I didn't want to be put out of the house I grew up in either.

"You don't have to worry about me, Daddy. I'll leave," Tori said, pulling away from Zach's grip. "I'd rather starve than to put my legs under the same table as this hussy."

"Toodles, Tori. Don't let the door hit you on the way out," I teased.

Mama didn't like my comment at all. "Dani, are you twenty-eight or just eight? When will you grow up? What you did was uncalled for and mean-spirited."

"Why is everybody coming down on me? All I did was ask a question. It isn't my fault Tori wasn't upfront with her fiancé."

Mama gave me a look of disdain and walked out the dining room. Kyle just sat back quietly and watched it all unfold. I could hear Daddy in the living room trying to stop Tori from leaving. Zach had finally followed behind Tori like a little trained puppy dog. Once things had gotten quiet again, I picked up my fork and shoved some potato salad in my mouth.

"Dani," Kyle whispered. "I thought you agreed to play fair today."

"You said that. I didn't."

Kyle just shook his head in disgust.

I didn't give a damn. I had come to eat and that I was gonna do. But just as I was about to bite into my fried drumstick, Tori stormed back into the dining and yelled, "I hope you choke, skank."

Before I could respond, she was gone. I was going to let her get away with the last word *this* time because I had already blown her out the water when I informed Zach that she was infertile. So, in my mind, I had won this battle. Now, I had to gear up for the next encounter—which I was certain was soon to come.

Chapter 8

Tori

"Tori, I need you to stop crying and talk to me," Zach demanded.

We had just left my parents house en route to my apartment and Zach wanted answers, but I was too upset to speak. As he drove, he started what felt like an interrogation.

"Do you hear me, Tori? I know you're upset, but we need to discuss what your sister said at dinner."

"Do we have to talk about it now?" I sobbed, my face buried in my hands.

"I think we do. I don't like the feeling of you keeping secrets from me with our wedding only a few months away. I've opened up about everything to you, and I expect you to do the same. So, you need to start talking. Now, can you explain to me what Dani was talking about? Is it true that you can't have children?"

I let out a long exasperated sigh. If I could've wrapped my hands around Dani's throat, I would have. It's because of her loose lips, I've now got to explain my medical history with Zach, something I never planned to do. I knew this was a selfish act, but I'd always been fearful that once I shared that I may not be able to conceive, he'd never want to marry me.

"Yes, Zach, it's true—somewhat."

"What? What do you mean 'it's true—somewhat?' Either you can have children or you can't? Which one is it?" Zach's tone was full of irritation. I wasn't used to him speaking to me like this, but I understood his frustration.

"Zach, a few years ago, I went to my gynecologist because I was suffering from heavy bleeding, cramping and pressure on my bladder. After an ultrasound examination, it was discovered that I had uterine fibroids. "

"What's that?" He frowned.

"It's real technical—something you probably won't understand."

"Try me. I'm not slow, ya know."

Zach had a real slick tongue at the moment. I was going to let him get away with it for now, but I'd be sure to pull him up about it later. "Fibroids are non-cancerous tumors that attach to the uterine wall. I had clusters of them in my uterus which ultimately affects my getting pregnant."

"So, why didn't you tell me this? Why did I have to hear it from Dani?"

"Because, although the chances of infertility are great in my case, it's not one hundred percent. My doctor has assured me that if I have fertility treatments there's a possibly that I could get pregnant. I've taken medication to shrink them, and I've been on birth control to help with the heavy bleeding. Things seem to be all right for now. I figured I could look into pregnancy options once we started discussing a family. We're still planning a wedding—children hasn't been a huge topic between us."

"You're right, but I'm still angered that you would keep something as important as this from me. I don't know what to think. Do you have any more secrets I should know about?"

"Oh stop it, Zach. You're taking this a bit too far. It's not that serious. I just told you having children is not totally out of the question, so what's the big deal?"

"The big deal is you didn't tell me about it in the first place. I'm disappointed and it makes me wonder."

"Wonder what?"

He didn't respond. Instead, he slowly pulled into the parking space in my apartment complex. "I'll call you later. I'm going home to clear my head."

"Are you serious? You're not even going to come in?"

He let out a fake yawn and said, "Naw. I'm tired. I'll give you a ring later this evening."

I just shook my head, opened the car door and exited the car. I slammed the door with much force so he'd know that I was angry as well. I stomped up the walkway to my apartment door, and before I could get my key in the door, he was gone. "Bastard," I mumbled as I entered my living room.

Denise Hawthorne, my best friend, sat in silence as she stared at me with her big brown eyes. Her look didn't faze me in anyway. It was two hours after Zach had dropped me off and I was still livid. I called Denise over to help calm my nerves, but it wasn't working. The anger that resided within me caused me to pace my living room floor wearing a hole in the plush carpet.

"Why you looking at me like that?" I asked, tired of her staring at me.

"I just think you need to calm down. Dani was wrong. I agree. But you getting all worked up about this isn't doing you any good. You need to focus on making amends with Zachary rather than how to get back at Dani."

"Whose side are you on? You're supposed to be my friend?"

"I am your friend. But as your friend, you know I don't bite my tongue, nor do I sugarcoat things for you," she snapped.

Denise was right. She was my best friend in the whole world. We'd been friends since junior high school. Denise and I were so close that she was more like a sister to me than Dani could ever be. Growing up we were inseparable. My parents even referred to her as their third child. With her honey-colored skin and short, naturally curly hair, she could have been a Prescott kid—the one in the middle—darker than me, but lighter than Dani. She'd been around for many years as I endured the harsh mistreatment by Dani. She knew firsthand how much of a low-down, backstabbing slut my sister really was.

Dani loathed Denise. She claimed Denise was just as much to blame for her suicide attempt as I was. Dani feels that we taunted her. I beg to differ. Her recollection of childhood events is totally distorted. Dani, Denise and I have had our heated moments and altercations, but we never said cruel things that would make her want to kill herself. Dani is delusional.

Denise wasn't lying when she said she never bit her tongue for me. That's what I loved about our friendship. She was going to tell me the truth no matter what, whether I liked it or not. Today, I needed her to be on my side. I didn't want her to play devil's advocate.

Trying to get Denise to see my side, I said, "Dani was wrong—dead wrong. It wasn't her place to say anything to Zach."

"That's why you should have told him a long time ago. I told you to tell him when he first proposed to you."

"I know Denise. I wish I had listened to you. Now the truth is out, and I'm sure we can work past this . . . but that . . . that . . . Dani . . . she's officially declared war."

"And just what are you gonna do, Tori?"

I rushed over to the cordless phone and snatched the handset off its base. "I'm gonna call her and give her a piece of my mind."

"What's that gonna solve? You'll only be stooping to her level. Stop to think: what would Jesus do in this situation?"

"Don't throw Jesus into this. I'm gonna do this and repent later." I dialed Dani's telephone number and Denise stood looking at me shaking her head. She knew not to try to intervene when I was on the rampage. It would only be a lost cause to do so when my mind was made up.

I tapped my foot on the floor as Dani's telephone rang. I waited impatiently for her to pick up. Finally, after four rings the voice mail picked up. I had to listen to the devil's fake, professional-sounding voice recording.

"*Hello. You have reached the Monroe residence. Sorry we're unable to take your call at the moment. Please leave a detailed message, and we'll be sure to return your call. Thanks and have a great day.*"

I was eager to hear the beep because I was about to let her have it on her voice mail. Beeeeeeeeeeeeeeeeeeeeeeeep. "You big-mouthed, backstabbing bitch. I can't believe you had the nerve to bring up my possible infertility to Zach. What the hell was your purpose? I can answer that for you. You're a miserable snake in the grass, and since you're not happy, you don't want anybody else to be happy. Don't try to make everybody's life unhappy because your baby died, which by the way was God's way of looking out for the fetus. He didn't want that child to be raised by a no-good, worthless piece of crap like you. And another thing, little sister, the next time you open up your mouth to say anything against me to my fiancé, I'm gonna put my fist in down your throat. Not a threat, but a promise."

I slammed the phone down. I turned to Denise who looked like she'd seen a ghost. I didn't care. I felt instant gratification and was thinking of calling back and telling her off some more.

Chapter 9

Mama

"Norm, what in God's name is wrong with your daughters?"

"Oh when they are acting like complete fools, they my daughters?"

"I just don't get it. Were they put on earth just to make each other miserable? I mean really. Think about it. What reason would Dani have to bring up Tori's inability to conceive at dinner today? What?"

"Baby, there ain't no reason. Dani was just being Dani. I wouldn't expect anything different."

"That's her problem. She thinks she can say and do things to people without regard of the outcome or people's feelings."

"That's the nature of her disability, Janice. That's also why Dani needs to be on her medication at all times. I don't know who she thinks she's fooling, but I know when she not taking her meds. Her attitude and demeanor tell it all."

"Yeah, like her flirting all up in Larry Johnson's face this morning—in the church at that."

"Oh but don't forget Larry was smiling like a Cheshire cat. He was engaged in the inappropriate behavior just as much as Dani was. I turned my head. I couldn't bare to watch them act as if they were single."

"Larry's been sweet on Dani for years. I don't think he's ever gotten over her. I know he moved on with his wife and new baby, but Larry ain't fooling me. He still cares a lot for Dani."

"I totally agree, Norm, but it was worse when Brendan slithered his way over to her. That boy was looking at her like he was going to start licking her face right in the sanctuary."

"By then, I wasn't in the mood to watch any more train wrecks, so I missed the show with Brendan. Was it that bad?"

"Yes, honey. It was *that* bad. Thank God Kyle was outside parking the car. I could only imagine what would've happened if he wasn't there today. I envisiond Dani and Brendan skipping church and getting a room somewhere."

Norm laughed.

"I'm serious. Dani disappoints me sometimes. She knows better."

"That's my point exactly. When she's not on her medication, she is unable to use good judgment, lacks concern for others and displays immoral behavior—like hitting on a married man in God's house."

"Well, I'mma talk to that girl about her meds. She needs them like yesterday. I don't like what I'm seeing as of late. And speaking of path. What was up with Tori today?"

"What do you mean?"

"She let Dani bring the ugly right out of her. I could tell the demons were having a good ole time with her today."

"Janice, Tori was hurt by what Dani revealed at dinner. I, too, was appalled. I think Tori's action was pretty normal. She's human, baby and humans have feelings."

"I understand that, I expect so much more from Tori. She knows Christ. She should handle situations with her sister a lot better than she does."

"I think you're asking a little bit too much of Tori. I don't agree with the manner in which things were handled today, but I can understand."

Well, Norm, we may have to agree to disagree on this subject. When a person knows Christ, they should represent Him at all times, even in the midst of conflict."

"Oh, please, Janice. And you've conducted yourself in a Christ-like manner in every argument or conflict you've ever had?"

I stood silent. Thinking. Thinking. Thinking. When I took too long to respond, Norm said, "Exactly. You are expecting things of Tori that you yourself don't do. Lighten up on the girl, please."

"OK, Norm. You've made your point. I'll cut Tori some slack on this one. But, she has to know Dani's disability will cause her to say mean, hurtful things."

"Sorry, Janice, I'm not giving Dani a free pass on this one. I have never been one to use her disability as crutch and I won't start today. Yes, I understand she reacts to things in an extreme manner, extremely up or extremely down, but what she did today was plain awful."

"You're right. I just hope they can get past this. This was serious. I wonder how Zach is taking the news about Tori not being able to have children."

"It was quite a shocker, I'm sure. But, I have faith, they'll get past it. Zach's a good man, a good God-fearing man, and I'm sure they can work it out. Now, Dani and Tori may be another issue altogether. They may need some time, like a year's time to heal after this latest episode."

"Don't say that, Norm. Now, you've got me all worried about them."

I took a deep breath as I eyed the telephone. "I'm gonna call them to check on them."

"No you are not. Let them be. They are grown. Let them fight their drama."

I didn't agree with Norm. As their parents I thought we should always intervene but since I shared a home, and bed with Norm, I thought it would be best to listen to his suggestion. I just prayed the girls were all right.

Chapter 10

Dani

"I'm gonna kill her," I bellowed as I threw the cordless phone on the bed. Kyle was on the other side of the bedroom changing his clothes when he heard my outburst.

He spun around and said, "What's wrong, Dani?"

Pounding my right fist into my left palm repeatedly, I responded, "Tori. I'm gonna kill her." My voice was trembling and my eyes welled with tears. Of all the things she could've said to me, making reference to my deceased child was totally out of order.

Confused, Kyle asked, "What'd she do now?"

"Can you believe she left a message on the voice mail talking about God allowing the baby to die because He didn't want our beloved son to be raised by a worthless piece of crap like me? Is she serious? That bitch must be crazy."

"Dani, you lying. Tori said that?"

"Yeah, she did. Listen to the message for yourself. I saved it."

Shaking his head in disbelief, he said, "Naw. I don't wanna hear no shit like that. The baby that died wasn't just your child. He was mine too, so I don't take comments like that lightly."

"Good. I'm glad we're on the same page. Then you'll understand why I'm on my way over to her apartment to kick her ass. I'm sick of this. She crossed the line this time, and now she's got to be dealt with."

Kyle walked over to me and wrapped his arms around me. "Baby, calm down. I know you're upset. I'm pissed the hell off, too, but going over to your sister's house to implement an ass whopping, although well deserved, is not the answer. You've gotta handle this better than that. You're an assistant principal remember? You've got to remain a productive citizen at all times because you never know when you'll run across your students and their parents. The last thing you want is for your face to be plastered all over the news. Baltimore doesn't need another scandal surrounding the school systems."

Pulling away from Kyle's grasp, I said, "Yeah, yeah, yeah. I heard all of what you just said, but I'm not feeling it. Besides, I'm on bereavement leave until the end of the summer."

"So, does that mean you put your career in jeopardy? Come on, Dani you're smarter than that."

Kyle seemed to be getting a bit irritated by my stance to get at Tori, but I didn't care. I was gonna pounce on her head whether he liked it or not, and I'd worry about the consequences later.

"Yep, I'm smart enough to know that my darling sister needs her ass kicked." I hurriedly slipped on a pair of jeans, gray t-shirt and gray and white New Balance gym shoes. I had to dress down in preparation to beat Tori down.

Kyle just stared at me in disbelief as if he couldn't believe I was actually going to take a chunk out of Tori's tail. I knew he was mad, but I didn't care. What I said about her infertility didn't begin to compare to the comments about my son's death. That was just unforgivable, and I was about to let her know it.

"Don't look at me like that. I gotta do what I gotta do. Sorry you don't like it, but I'm out." I didn't give him a chance to say a word. I walked out the bedroom and slammed the door behind me before he could even speak. I rushed down the stairs of our townhouse, grabbed my purse and keys off the dining room table and made a mad dash for the front door. It was about to be on!

Chapter 11

Tori

I eagerly answered the phone when I looked at the caller ID, and it displayed Dani's number. I had been waiting for her to call me all evening. I knew her well and that message would definitely cause her to go off the deep end—just the effect I desired.

Her calling me now, excited me because I was ready to give her a piece of my mind.

"What?" I shouted in the phone.

"Tori?" A male voice responded.

It wasn't Dani. It was Kyle. Damn. "What do you want, Kyle?"

"Why are you being so short with me? Have I done something to you?"

"Kyle, let's not even go there, OK? Just think back to the day you started dating my sister, and that alone should answer your question."

"Look, I didn't call to get into it with you. Although I am messed up with you after you called here with that bullshit, I just wanted to give you a heads up that Dani is livid over that wicked ass voice mail you left. She stormed out of the house with fire shooting from her ears. She's on her way over there to confront you."

"Oh, really. Well, I gladly welcome my sister dearest to come over. I've got a few things I want to say to her as well."

"I don't think you understand. Dani's not coming to talk. She's coming over for a brawl. She said she's coming to beat you down."

"Ha," I laughed. "Then tell her to come on."

"Tori, somebody's gotta be the bigger person here. I'm calling because I couldn't talk some sense into Dani before she stormed out of the house. I was hoping to get through to you. When she shows up, can you please just not open the door? I don't want y'all to do this. You're too old to be fighting."

"Kyle, if Dani wants to bring it, then I'm gonna let her. And I'll be ready, willing and waiting to put her in ICU."

"But Tori—"

"Thanks for the heads up. I'm hanging up now. I need to take off my earrings and put some Vaseline on my face to protect myself from scratches."

"This isn't a joke, Tori. This is serious."

"Bye, Kyle."

When I hung up, my heart raced with adrenaline. I welcomed Dani to show up at my door. I wasn't scared of her. She was more bark than bite. But best believe I would be the one biting tonight. Dani had successfully ruined a nice dinner and blurted out my personal business to Zach which had caused a division in our relationship. Oh yeah, it was on for sure. I anticipated her visit with glee.

* * *

I sat in my living room, flipping through the latest edition of Ebony Magazine waiting for Dani's arrival. She never came. After looking at the clock, which read 8:15 P.M., I knew she wasn't coming. She only lived twenty minutes from me. If she were coming, she would've been here already.

I decided to prepare for the start of a new work week. I ironed my clothes, packed my lunch and thought a lot about Zach. He hadn't called since he dropped me off hours before. I wondered if he was still angry. I picked up the phone several times to dial his number, but quickly hung it up again. I didn't really know what to say. I guess an apology would be the best way to start off the conversation.

I picked up the phone once again to call Zach. I dialed his home number at first. The phone rang four times before his answering machine picked up. "That's odd," I spoke aloud. "I don't recall there being any church functions this evening. Wonder where he is? Maybe he's just ignoring my calls."

I attempted to call his cell phone. No answer. But this time, I left a message. "Hi, Zach. It's me. When you get a chance, please call me. I really want to talk to you. I don't like how we left things earlier, and I want to talk about it. Please call me as soon as you get this message. Love you."

When I hung up, I felt uneasy. I had a funny feeling he was purposely ignoring my phone calls. This was one thing I detested about him. Zach could be one tough cookie. He wasn't always easy to forgive. This personality trait stemmed from childhood. His parents divorced when he was a young boy and his father made lots of empty promises to him throughout his life which has affected him today. His mother struggled to raise two boys, Zach and his brother, Darren as their father was barely around. Zach's dad was involved in numerous extramarital affairs which led him to be away from home, his wife and children. When he was around, he would often promise to buy them toys, clothes, send money, take them on trips and a bunch of other empty promises, but he never followed through. By the time, Zach reached his late teens, he had grown to resent his father and had developed serious trust issues. I believe his childhood was another reason he latched on to young children as a counselor and youth minister. He wanted to be a saving grace for them. But in all honesty, Zach might've been the one who needed the counseling. His lack of trust for people seriously needed to be addressed. I guess my keeping the infertility issue from him just added me to the list of people he couldn't trust anymore. *God, how I wish I could do it all over again.*

Moments after leaving the message for Zach, my phone rang. "Hello?"

"Tori, it's Kyle. Is everything all right over there?" he asked nervously.

Disappointed to hear Kyle's voice and not Zach, I sighed, "Kyle, Dani never came over here. She was just talkin' foolishly."

"That's strange. She was adamant that she was coming over there. I've been sitting here debating if I should come over to your place or not."

"No need. She ain't come, and I'm about to get ready to go to bed. I've got work tomorrow unlike Dani."

"Tori. You know Dani is on bereavement leave. If she wasn't she'd be going to work tomorrow, too."

"Yeah, yeah, yeah. Tell it to somebody who really cares."

"I'm so surprised at you lately, Tori. You just seem to

be different—not the nice church-going young lady I used to know. Quite frankly, your attitude sucks."

"My attitude sucks? You've got to be kidding me. Let me tell you what sucks. When your ex-boyfriend, whom you loved dearly, dates, impregnates and marries your sister. That sucks. When your so-called sister blurts out at a family dinner that you're unable to conceive a child, that sucks. So, yeah, my attitude is nasty but I've always maintained that when it comes to Dani and her foolishness, the church-going young lady becomes consumed with anger and hate."

"How many times do I have to say sorry for everything that has happened? I never meant to hurt you."

"Kyle, I don't want to rehash all of this. It is what it is, and I'm learning to live with it, but you can't expect me not to have some ill feelings toward you both for it. I may love the Lord, but I ain't perfect."

"Was it your ill feelings that caused you to leave such a depraved message on our voice mail about the baby? I was really surprised when Dani told me about it, and a little hurt, too."

"It wasn't meant to hurt you, Kyle. I was angry. Probably wasn't the right thing to do, but oh well. What's done is done . . . just like you marrying my sister."

"Wow. I see you're really bitter. When are you gonna just let this all go? Aren't you getting married soon?"

"Whatever, Kyle. If you say, I'm bitter, then so be it. I'm bitter. All I've ever wanted was to co-exist on this earth with Dani without all the nonsense. She seems to make it her mission to make my life hell and then when I react to it, everybody is so surprised at Little Miss Christian Tori. I'm sorry, but I'm human and a person can only take but so much.

I'm fed up with Dani. It's to the point where I never want to see her again. She's done too much damage for me to ever accept her into my life again. I just want to be finished with her. And if God doesn't understand that, then I'm sorry."

"I understand that you've been dealing with Dani's stuff for years now, hell all your life, and I hope that both of you will eventually find some peace. I don't like seeing you like this . . . I'm not used to it and honestly, I don't like it. I want to be in the presence of good-girl Tori." He laughed.

"Well, just pray for me. I'm still a good girl, except when it comes to Dani. That's where my other personality kicks in."

"Alrighty then. I guess I'll call Dani on her cell phone. I have no idea where she is."

"You do that. I'm off to bed."

"Have a good night's rest. I'll speak to you soon. Goodnight."

Actually, I hoped to not be speaking with Kyle soon. We really had nothing to talk about. My issues with him were just as significant as they were with Dani. Besides, Kyle wasn't the man I wanted to talk to. It was Zach. It bothered me that I still hadn't heard from him. I debated if I should call him again. Instead, I just decided to pray about it.

I lay my head on my fluffy pillow and closed my eyes. I couldn't shake this uneasy feeling I had about my relationship with Zach being in trouble. I hoped I was overacting, but my gut told me that I just might have lost him. I decided to have a long conversation with God because I knew He could ease my troubled soul.

Chapter 12

Dani

He planted his lips on mine. His tender kiss ignited my fire as I lay on my back, inviting him to mount me, to make love to me.

Slow and sensual, he moved inside me. Then I rolled on top of him. He slowly guided his manhood into my vaginal tunnel. I immediately began to ride him like a bucking bronco. Our eyes were locked and fixed on each other as we explored each other's bodies and needs. I felt him and he felt me and then we both exploded in ecstasy.

Panting and sweating profusely, my secret lover, rolled over and said, "You know we shouldn't be doing this."

I smiled. I knew his conscience would eventually get the best of him, but I didn't care. The minute I laid eyes upon him in church, I knew I'd be clawing at his back again—within hours. "Why not? Wasn't it just as good for you as it was for me?"

"Oh, yes. It's always good. I'm never dissatisfied when I have you in my bed, but this is wrong. You and I both know."

"So, you're feeling guilty now?" I said running my foot seductively up and down his thigh.

"I do. I shouldn't be doing this. I'm engaged to your sister."

"So what, Zach. You and Tori aren't married yet? It's OK to have a little fun until she puts that ring on your finger."

"But you're married. So, no matter how you look at it, we're wrong . . . dead wrong."

"Please, Zach. Let's not kill the mood. You've been tapping my booty for over a year. So, don't develop a conscience now."

I'd met Zach at one of my mother's famous dinner parties that she had for no special occasion. He was introduced to me as Tori's co-worker and friend. I knew from the way she was sticking to him like glue that he was more than a friend. This revelation alone caused me to put a plan into motion to get at him. Not because I wanted him for myself, but because I was on a constant mission to derail Tori's life like she had done mine. Taking, yet another one of her men, would do my heart some good.

At first, I had to feel him out. It wasn't easy getting him away from Tori, at the party, but I swooped in when I saw him at the table pouring another cup of Mommy's famous punch. Subtly, I moved over to him to find out if he was like most guys, swayed by a pretty smile, a protruding cleavage and a plump booty. After only minutes of conversing with him, I could tell he would be easier than expected. The fact that we both were involved with the school system and working with children opened up the door for me. It was then I planted the seed that I wanted to bed him. I cleverly told him that one night with me, would make him wish I was the sister he met first. He didn't jump at my advances, but he didn't seem disturbed by them either. I waited a couple of weeks to see if I'd hear from Tori—meaning that he'd told her what I said. I never heard from her.

Finally, I looked up his email address in the school system's global address list. I sent him a "Nice to meet you" message. He responded with a "likewise" message, but didn't say enough for me to catch if he was feeling where I was trying to go with this thing.

Ironically, a month later, I ran into him at a statewide educational conference in Montgomery County, Maryland and my flirtatious instincts went into overdrive. I asked him out to lunch, he agreed and from there our fling was launched.

Zach and I cared for each other, but we weren't in love. We've never discussed being a couple. It was just all fun and games and sweet revenge on my part.

Honestly, Zach, had never been proud of our "relationship." He'd always felt some guilt because of it, but he was totally addicted to my adventurous bedroom nature, something that was nonexistent with Tori. He threatened to end our relationship every other month, but I always found my way back into his mind and bedroom.

"It's just that when we started this, you weren't married to Kyle, just dating him. I wasn't engaged to Tori. Since then, you've gotten pregnant, then married and I proposed to Tori. I also wasn't the youth minister at the church. Things are different now. We both have a lot to lose."

"Please. The only two people who know are in this room right now. Who's gonna tell Tori, Kyle or even Pastor Brice about us? As long as you keep your mouth shut, things will be fine."

"Me keep my mouth shut? I'm able to do that. But can you? I'm constantly anxious about what's gonna slip out of your mouth when you're battling with Tori. I'm on edge wondering if you're gonna tell her about us just to stab her in the heart."

"Oh, please Zach. I ain't crazy enough to mess up a good

thing. I like what we have. Why do you think I told Kyle the baby was his?"

"Well, it was his baby. We always use protection, so I knew the baby wasn't mine."

"I guess we'll never know now will we?" I said, falling into a somber mood. Just thinking about the loss of the baby saddened me.

Zach must have noticed my high spirits decline immediately. "Come here." He said, wrapping his arms around my naked body. "It's gonna be alright. You'll get pregnant again. You'll have a baby. I'm sure of it."

"Do you want to be the father?" I joked.

"Stop playing, Dani. I'm about to marry your sister. At some point this relationship is gonna have to end."

"Why? It doesn't have to end if you don't want it to."

"Yes, it does. I feel like such a hypocrite standing before the youth, telling them how to conduct themselves, and here I am, engaged to a woman but sleeping with her married sister. You have no idea how guilt consumes me. Besides, I'm afraid of the wrath of God. I know my consequences are coming soon. I'm trying to brace myself for it."

"Oh, Zach, give me a break. You ain't going nowhere. I'll be right up in your bed once you say 'I do' to Tori. You're addicted to this," I said, running his hand against my female sex organ.

"Doubt me if you will, but this will be the last time we see each other like this. We just have to."

"Whatever. That's what your lips say. Anyway, since this is our *last* night together, I just wanted to thank you for helping me through the loss of the baby. It's been good knowing I had your shoulder to lean on."

"No problem. I wish I could've been there more, but you understand why I couldn't."

"Yeah, yeah, whatever. So, when are you going to call Tori? I know she's probably crying by now since you haven't returned her calls."

"I'll stop by her classroom tomorrow to speak to her. I'm still upset about the infertility thing. I wish she would've told me. But in light of all I've done to her, I can forgive her for that. At least she's not sleeping with my brother."

"Stop beating yourself up. We *all* sin daily. Just repent and move on."

"It's not that easy, Dani. When you repent, you should go humbling before God asking for his forgiveness with the intention of not repeating that same act again. In the past, I couldn't, but maybe since things are going to be over between us after tonight, I can ask God to forgive me."

I chuckled. I ignored his comments about our relationship being over. Granted, it was just hot, steamy sex between us— no love or nothing—but I knew what I was giving him, Tori wasn't, and because of that fact alone, I knew it wasn't over between us. But, I'd keep letting him try to convince himself.

"So, was dinner at my parents' house off the hook or what?"

"Dani, you know you didn't have to throw Tori under the bus like that. You could have told me in private or allowed Tori to tell me."

"Honestly, I thought you knew. I was really just trying to throw it up in her face that she couldn't have children. I didn't know I was revealing Tori's best kept secret."

"Well, you did. It caught me totally off guard, and she was really hurt."

"Oh, so what. I don't want to talk about her anymore. Since, you say, this is our last night together, let's make our remaining moments memorable. I gotta get home before Kyle sends the FBI out looking for me."

Zach chuckled. "Yeah, he's probably wondering if you're in jail by now for going to battle with Tori. And if he knows that you never showed up at her apartment, you'll have some 'splainin' to do."

"Well, I'll think of some lie on the way home. I'll tell him I was with Capri or somewhere trying to clear my head. But, um, enough about our significant others already. You owe me one more blissful climax."

Playing the role of reluctance, Zach sighed as if he was unsure if we should be intimate again. But, I wasn't waiting for him to respond. I was gonna have some fun whether he liked it or not.

Once I mounted him, his lack of enthusiasm miraculously disappeared. As always, he gave in to his flesh and lust and went along for the ride—enjoying our *final* rendezvous.

Chapter 13

Mama

Two days after that dreadful Sunday dinner I invited the girls over for a talk. I couldn't hold my peace any longer and needed to give the twins a stern talking to.

Tori slightly snarled at me when she heard, Dani's voice coming through the front door of my home.

"Ma," she whispered. "Why didn't you tell me she was going to be here?"

"'Cause I knew you wouldn't come. Now, sit your behind down and act like you've got some sense."

Dani entered the family room where Tori and I were sitting. She stopped abruptly when she saw Tori seated in the reclining chair.

"Come on in," I waved. "Have a seat, and stop looking like you've seen a ghost."

"I have," Dani snapped.

"Dani, quit it. I'm telling you and Tori right now, I am not for the bickering today. I'm not, and so help me God, if I have to smack some sense into one or both of you, I will."

"Sorry, Ma," Dani said. "But, I don't feel comfortable being in the same room with the person who left a voice mail message stating she was glad my baby died."

Tori spat, "I did not say that. Stop twisting my words."

"Well, what did you say? You said God did the baby a favor by killing him—"

Tori screamed, "You lying sack of —"

"Stop it. Stop it, right now," I shouted, clenching my chest. It felt like a knife had pierced my heart for thirty seconds. "Don't you two ever get tired of this fussing and fighting? Don't you get tired of this back and forth, constant bickering? Don't you get tired of walking around with all this hatred, bitterness and malice in your hearts? Aren't you worn out from being mad all the time? You two are a disappointment to your father and me. We never would have guess that the babies we prayed for would turn out like this. You girls have given us more grief than we ever imagined, and I'm sick of it. Your father is sick of it. We can't invite our two children to our home at the same time without feeling the next World War is about to break out. When you're around, we feel uncomfortable and increased tension in our own home. That's just ridiculous. And this is the reason I called you over here today. Truthfully, I am fed-up with you, Tori, and I am fed-up with you, Dani. Thinking about the way my twin girls behave is nauseating and today I want to work toward a resolution. So, sit down and shut up. I'm calling the shots up in my house today, and if you don't like it, you can get out."

I paused to see if either of them were bold enough to go against me. I didn't get fired up often, but they had succeeded in bringing out the witch in me. With both Tori and Dani seated, and with their mouths closed for once, I began telling them the purpose of the meeting.

"Girls, I called you both here today because I want us to begin working toward healing this broken relationship between you two. I heard all about the message and the baby comment that Tori made. I heard all about you, Dani, threatening to go Tori's house to 'beat her down.' I'm guessing this all stemmed from the revelation Dani made at Sunday dinner about Tori not being able to have children."

"How'd you hear about what happened after we left,Mama?" Dani asked.

Sarcastically, I responded, "I've got my sources. People keep me in the loop and that's all you need to know."

Dani chuckled. "Okay, you can protect sources, but I'm quite sure it was Kyle."

"Anywaaaaaaaaaaay," I said, rolling my eyes. "After I heard about this latest bunch of mess, I sought the Lord on how I should handle it. For years, your father has been telling me to leave it alone, to let you girls be, but I can't. This drama between you two is literally making me ill."

Tori gasped. "What do you mean, 'making you ill'?"

"Well, for the last two months, I've noticed that whenever I get a call informing me that you two are at it again or when I witness it for myself, I instantly get chest pains."

Concerned, Dani said, "What kind of chest pains, Mama? Are they really bad? Do you need to see a doctor?"

"No, I have not been to the doctor. It's not an on-going thing. I'm telling you, it only happens when you two are actively engaged in combat." I paused as I tried to fight crying, but to no avail. "Girls, I think I'm suffering from a broken heart."

Tori rushed to my side. She kneeled on the floor beside my chair and said, "Awwwwww, Mama. Don't cry. I'm sorry. I'm sorry for putting you through all of this."

"Well, baby. Until you are a mother, you'll never know

how awful it feels to have your only two children in the world consistently in warfare. I'll put it to you this way, imagine a mother having two sons, being told that both her children were being sent to war in Iraq. Imagine how that mother would feel each day wondering if her children are okay, if they'd been hurt, if they were still alive, if she'd ever see them again. That's excruciating pain to the tenth power."

Dani finally chimed into the conversation. "But, Mama, despite the differences between Tori and me, you have to know that we both love you dearly. There's nothing in the world we wouldn't do for you."

"You don't understand. All I've ever wanted was for my girls to have a simple sibling bond. Hell, I'm not even asking for you to be inseparable, but at least make an attempt to be cordial, to get along well enough to have a nice family dinner, to attend a church service without animosity floating in the air, to call one another just to say hi. Is it really that hard? I mean really?"

Tori and Dani sat with blank stares. I was hoping deep down, I was really getting to them. But, just in case I wasn't, I needed to keep pouring guilt into their souls. "Was I a bad mother to y'all or something?"

"Mama, no," Dani said, clearly taken aback by my comment. "You cannot blame yourself for what's happened with us. It's not your fault."

"It's got to be. I keep wondering if it was something I could have done when y'all were babies that could have made you turn out differently. I beat myself up all the time questioning if it was my parenting skills or lack thereof that impeded the two of you from having a stronger bond. Was it something

I did during the pregnancy? Was something in the Simalac? Did I not show enough love and affection? Did I make one feel inferior over the other? Clearly, something had to have gone wrong for y'all to carry such disdain in your hearts toward each other."

"You cannot blame yourself for any of this, Mama. I don't think we could have predicted childhood sibling rivalry would have spilled over into adulthood," Tori spoke.

Dani chimed in, "I agree with you, Mama. It should not have gone this far, but I refuse to allow you to carry the blame for the things we do. And no matter what, you were and are a great mother to us and we love you for it."

"If you truly loved me, you wouldn't be breaking my heart like this. I'm in pain girls, literally in pain, and it's you that's causing it. I keep hoping and praying that before I close my eyes and leave this earth, you two will have enough sense to love each other as siblings and stop all this nonsense. My biggest fear with death is knowing I may never see you two make amends. If only you were a mother, then maybe you'd understand how I feel." I cried and grabbed my chest as one of those pains passed through my heart again.

Tori noticed my anguish and held me. "Mama, are you all right? Is it happening again?"

Sitting back in the chair, I spoke softly, "Yeah, that was another one. But, I'm fine now. It's gone."

"Mama, I'm really concerned. You need to see a doctor," Dani said with fright in her eyes.

"Didn't I just tell you there is nothing a doctor can do to cure my pains? What can he give me for a broken heart? Huh?"

"You assume it's a broken heart, but you don't really know," Dani asserted. "You need to make an appointment ASAP."

"I'll look into it, Dani. But, in the meantime, can the two of you work toward just a small resolution? Can we cease fire for just a little while?"

"I'm open for it, Mama." Tori confirmed. "This situation has taken a toll on me as well and all for what? Each time I find myself more and more out of the will of God when engaging in these futile, immature battles with Dani. It's also not healthy. So, I'm open to calling it quits. I think everything else will have to take some time. A lot of damage has been done."

Dani sat with her arms crossed. She was silent. It looked as if she was contemplating whether to end the petty battles with Tori. I knew she'd be the hardest to persuade, but I couldn't stop trying. I needed to get through to her.

"Dani, sweetheart. Tori is willing. What about you?" Still no response. "Honey, I'm not asking you to jump right into a sisterly relationship. All I'm asking is that you both agree to stop with the arguing, fussing, name calling, threats, the nasty messages, the not-so-subtle attempts to drop private information about one another and all the other hateful things you've been doing. I just want my children to co-exist in my home without your father and me feeling uncomfortable. Am I asking too much?"

I could see Dani softening, but she still struggled to give in. "Well, Dani? Can you do it at least for me? For my aching heart?"

"Yes, Mama," she whispered. "I can do it for you. Because I love you and respect you, I will end this mess with Tori today. But, at this point, don't expect much more from me. Let me take my time with this. I can't let go of years of hurt in just one conversation."

"I'm just asking for you to take baby steps, my dear. Right now a cease fire is the best news I've received in years. I love both you girls. I really do. I can't thank you enough for agreeing to help me work on healing my broken heart. Now, Dani get over here and give me and your sister a hug."

Dani was reluctant at first, but she honored my request. When the three of us embraced, I felt my heart dancing. It was like it was instantly healed.

Chapter 14

Tori

I was at home, filled with an array of emotions. I was upset about the meeting at my mother's house. I felt horrible after learning she'd been having chest pains potentially caused by Dani and me. Also, the fact that I had still had not had a civilized conversation with Zach since last Sunday, was maddening. I was heated with him for acting so immaturely about this whole thing. Ignoring my phone calls and being distant was so beneath him, so I thought. I had intended to call him on his actions today, but the meeting at Mama's house and her being ill took priority over me giving Zach a good tongue lashing. I'd plan to address it later.

I sat at the foot of my bed, contemplating if I should reach out to Zach again. His recent actions made me hesitant, but I decided to give him a call anyway.

Tearfully, I said, "Zach. Where are you?"

"I'm on my way to the church for a ministry meeting with Pastor Brice. What's wrong?"

"I need you right now. I just left my parents' house. My mother duped Dani and me into coming over so she could talk to us. It seems we're breaking her heart and—"

"And what?" he asked, voice filled with alarm.

"And after Mama's heartfelt talk about wanting us to be cordial to one another and to stop the beefin', I was really ready to give in. I was genuinely ready to give up this constant fighting with Dani."

"Well, what's stopping you? You are in control of you. If you want to end this fued, you can."

"It's Dani. She's a mean and hateful wench."

"Tori, watch what you're saying. Those words are not of God."

"I know this, Zach. But, it's the truth. After my mother cried her eyes out, explained that we were literally breaking her heart and enlightened us as to how our behavior and actions were affecting her physically, we agreed to end the fighting."

"You're losing me here. What physical pain is your mother enduring? I still don't see the issue. If you've agreed to stop fighting, why are you upset?"

I got a tab bit testy with Zach. I felt like he was interrogating me more than comforting me. I felt like the conversation was going no where fast.

"Mama said she's been suffering from chest pains for the last two months. She explained that these pains only come about when Dani and I are at odds."

"Well, then it seems like you and Dani need to call it quits for your mom. It's not farfetched for parents to grieve over stuff like this. I've seen it many times. Parents, especially mothers, will blame themselves for any and everything that happens to their children. Your mother has taken on this war between her daughters as if it were her own battle to fight.

She's probably internalized it more than she's realized, and now it's messing with her royally."

"Wow. You hit it right on the head. She told us, she blames herself, but we tried to reassure her that none of this is her fault."

"You expressing that to her isn't going to help. She'll only feel better about all of this if and when she sees a change between you and Dani. I agree. Y'all too old for this stuff. I think I could handle it better if y'all just didn't talk. This plotting and backstabbing is out of control."

Offended by Zach's use of the word y'all when referring to plotting and backstabbing, I firmly stated, "I do not plot or backstab Dani. Anything I do to her is in retaliation for something evil she's done to me. I do not scheme and design plans to bring her down. She does that. Not me. So, don't say, y'all," I screamed.

"Tori, you're not innocent in this stuff at all. Do you think just because you act out of retaliation, it makes you better than Dani? When you stoop to her level, it makes you look just as bad if not worse. At least she's not walking around with a Bible in her hand, professing her love for Jesus Christ all the while conjuring up ways to even the score."

"How dare you, Zachary Ambrose? I'm so sick of you taking her side every time this subject comes up. I'm fed up with you condemning me for being human. Show me a perfect Christian, and I'll show you Satan's palatial mansion in heaven. Until then, you don't have a right to judge me . . . at all."

In a more sensitive tone, Zach responded, "I'm not judging you, Tori. I'm just trying to help you understand that in order for this situation to change with you and Dani, maybe you're the one who needs to do the changing. Maybe you're the one who needs to be the bigger person. Obviously, she's not making an attempt. So, the modified behavior should start with you. Why don't you model the behavior you desire from her?"

"Ugh. Must you use that counseling banter with me right now?"

"Ahhhhh, yes, ma'am. I'm a counselor twenty-four/seven. But seriously, think about what I've said. Get into your Word. It's soothes the soul. Just think how things could have been different had you read a few scriptures about forgiveness instead of calling Dani's home, leaving that hurtful message about the baby."

I swallowed hard. I never wanted Zach to know I made that call to Dani. I knew he'd be all over me the moment he found out. I was popped like a thief in the night. If only he could've seen my face. Deer in headlights described it perfectly. But, um, how did he find out if I didn't tell him?

"Okay, Zach that was wrong. I'll admit it. I was angry. But, I have a question for you. How did you know about the message to Dani?" Silence. I knew he was still on the other end of the phone because I could still hear background noises. "Hello? Zach?"

"Yeah?"

"Did you hear me?"

"Naw, baby. What'd you say? My phone is losing its signal."

"How did you know about that message I left on Dani's voice mail?"

"I-I-I just know. God reveals things, ya know?" He chuckled.

"Oh, so you're a prophet now? Your spiritual oneness with God has increased to the level of now knowing who I call and the messages I leave, huh?"

"Girl, you're funny. Look. I'm pulling into the church parking lot now. We can finish this conversation later. It seems to me that you and Dani can work this thing out. Just put pride aside and think of your parents, especially your mother."

"That's easier said than done, Zach. Dani doesn't want to resolve this."

Zach huffed. "What makes you say that?"

"Because, after we talked, Mama asked us to hug and when we did, Dani leaned over Mama's shoulder and mouthed, 'I hate your guts.' Mama didn't hear her, but I read her lips. That's why I'm so upset. This mess is never ending, and I'm sick of it."

"Tori, babe. I've got to make this meeting, but we will continue this later. I'll call you on my way home from church. Maybe I can bring you a hot fudge Sundae to calm your spirit. We can pray together, discuss our upcoming nuptials, anything to make you feel better. OK?"

I smiled. "OK, my darling. I look forward to that. Tell Pastor Brice, I said hello."

"Will do. I love you, Tori."

"I love you back."

Chapter 15

Dani

"Hey, Kyle."

"Dani? Where are you? I've been waiting for you to get home. What was so urgent with your mother?"

"I know. I'm sorry. That's why I'm calling. I'll be home later. I'm going over to sit with Capri for a while. I just wanna cry on her shoulder for a bit."

"Why? What happened?"

"It's Mama. She made me feel like shit this afternoon. She basically said that my actions toward Tori are breaking her heart. She's suffering from chest pains and everything. It's really bothering me."

"Wow. I'm so sorry to hear that. Why don't you come home? We can talk more about it. Let me comfort you?"

Good thing Kyle couldn't see my face because I frowned at the thought of him comforting me. Sadly, he was the last person I wanted to console me.

"I'll be home later, Kyle. Let me talk to Capri first and then I'll be there."

"Dani, you do realize that I'm your husband, right?"

"What?" I snapped. "Where is that coming from?"

"I'm just saying, you're in the street more than you're home. And when you're home we barely talk let alone make love. Now, you claim to be feeling gloomy after talking with your mom today, but you're running to your friend, Capri for soothing. Am I missing something here? Is there something you want to tell me? I'm a grown man. I can take it."

I could tell Kyle was deeply irritated with me. But, I wasn't moved by the dissatisfaction in his voice. I, too, was grown and didn't have to answer to him. "It's not even like that, Kyle. Capri and I had made plans to do lunch today, but because I stayed with my mother longer than expected, I just told her I'd come by later this evening. It's just a coincidence that the stuff with Mama happened today. And I do realize you're my husband, that's why I'm explaining this much to you. Understand, that if there was something I needed to tell you, I'd tell you. You know I don't bite my tongue. So, if there was something you needed to know, you'd know."

"Whatever, Dani. You're on some ole ill shit right now. We'll talk about this when you get home. It's almost seven o'clock. Can I expect you home before midnight? Since you've been on leave, you don't seem to get home before midnight, and that's unacceptable. Grown woman or not, it's down right disrespectful."

"O-O-OK, Kyle," I answered. I was distracted by the sight of Zachary standing in the living room window of his apartment, shirtless. His pectoral muscles, well-developed biceps and six-pack abdomen were screaming for me to get off the phone with Kyle and come in to get a closer view. "I'll be home before midnight. Actually, I'll be home before nine. I promise."

"Yeah, aiight."

Giving in to Kyle was the easiest way to shut him up. I've mastered the art of getting over on him so well, and he didn't even realize it. I can't say it enough...he's such a sucker. If only he was a real man. And speaking of a real man, Mr. Zachary Ambrose was patiently waiting for me. Yes, he said the last time was the last time, but it didn't take much to convince him to go back on that "agreement" when I told him I was feeling little depressed today and wanted to be held. He was eager to oblige and now I was getting ready let him stroke my wounds.

"My, God, Dani. This really has to stop," Zachary spoke while gasping for air. "My wedding is weeks away, and I can't keep sleeping with you. This is shameful, disrespectful and sinful. We know better. And when one knows better, they should do better."

"Zach, please don't start having a conscience now. What's done is done. We can't undo what we just did, and what we will continue to do."

He snickered. "Continue to do? Now, that's where you're wrong, my sister. This can't continue. I'm really starting to feel bad about this. Tori loves me. We have an almost perfect relationship. Our only issues are surrounding you and this war you two declared. She's a good woman Dani and I can't keep doing this to her."

I wasn't the least bit fazed by Zach's comments about Tori and his relationship with her. I didn't care. If only I had a dime for every time he said he was going to end our physical relationship, I'd be able to afford Michael Jackson's

Neverland Ranch. Zach was full of it. He knew, and I knew it. So, instead of engaging him in the conversation, I rolled out of bed, wrapped my bare body in a bathrobe and went to the kitchen to pour myself a glass of wine. On second thought, I'd planned to pour myself several glasses of wine because I could feel a lecture brewing.

"You want some?" I held my glass, offering him a sip of my drink.

"No. I have work in the morning. Unlike you."

"Cheap shot, Zach. You know I'm on bereavement leave. I'm not going back to work anytime soon. Besides, the school year is coming to an end. Summer vacation is around the corner so I'll return once the kids have left."

"Well, since you've taken the liberty to pour yourself a glass of my wine, let me ask you this. Why did you tell Tori you hated her guts today at your mom's house? Why would you tell your mom you wanted to end the feuding if you never intended to do so?"

"Ugh. There you go. This ain't no therapy session, Zach," I spoke emphatically. "I don't wanna talk about that high-yella heifer, Tori. But, I will say this, that hussy told me the feeling was mutual after I told her I hated her guts. I bet she ain't tell ya that."

"It doesn't matter. Both of y'all are wrong and—"

I needed to shut him up like I did Kyle. But, with Zach it wasn't as easy as agreeing with him. I had to do something to him physically since that was our major connection. I stuck my tongue in his mouth and kissed him passionately to get him to stop with the lecturing. As always, it worked. And that kiss led to another round of wrestling in the sheets. Not another word was spoken about us ending our relationship or his stank ass fiancée. However, the bed activity coupled with the wine engulfed me with exhaustion. I needed to take a quick nap before going home. It was almost ten thirty. I was already late. I knew Kyle was pissed. I readjusted my thinking and strived to make it home by midnight. Zach said he'd be up watching *ESPN* News and promised to wake me up in an hour so I could make my way home. A few minutes later, I feel into a deep sleep.

Chapter 16

Tori

It was seven in the morning when the earsplitting sound of my ringing telephone disrupted my sleep and the quietness of my home. Instantly, I was perturbed that someone was calling so early on my day off. Being caught up with wedding planning, the everyday trials of working with children and the drama surrounding my personal life, afforded me the gift of taking a mental health day. I had purposely chosen a Friday to ensure a three-day weekend. I had my day all mapped out. I wasn't going to roll out of bed until ten o'clock. Then I'd trot into the kitchen to make a cup of cappuccino. And while sipping on my drink, I'd read my Daily Word message and afterwards, I'd do nothing.

I wasn't even going to make plans to see Zach. I was slightly ticked with him for not calling me when he got home the night before as he promised. After talking at length about what occurred at my mother's house, I felt somewhat better. He'd always been good at calming my spirit. But, it angered me when he didn't keep his promises, especially something as small as a phone call once he walked through his front door. Zach knew his voice was the last thing I needed to hear each night. He robbed me of that, not to mention a few other times in recent weeks. This was starting to become habitual, and I didn't like it. And for this reason, I refused to pick up the phone to call him.

The weather man predicted a beautiful, sunny May day. I opened my living room curtains to allow the sunlight to brighten my home. I thought of doing some cleaning, but quickly dismissed the notion. The objective for the day was to chilax—chill and relax. But it seemed someone had different plans for me.

"Hello," I whispered, to make the caller aware that I was sleeping. Hopefully, they'd get the message and decide not to hold a lengthy conversation.

"Tori, I'm sorry to wake you, but I'm worried about Dani?'

"Kyle?"

Speaking in a fast-paced, panicky tone he responded, "Yeah, it's me. Dani didn't come home last night, and I can't reach her on her cell. Do you have any idea where she may be?"

"No disrespect, Kyle, but why would I know Dani's whereabouts? Are you sure you meant to call me and not Capri?"

"I called Capri, but she's not answering either. I'm really worried, Tori."

"Well, Kyle, I can't help you. I have no clue. Have you called Mama or Daddy? They may know something."

"I didn't call your parents because I didn't want to upset them or get them all in an uproar about this. I thought maybe you would've talked to your parents this morning and they possibly mentioned something."

"Nope. I haven't talked to my folks." Wanting to return to sleep, I offered a suggestion, "How about I give you a call if I hear anything?"

"Thanks, Tori. Please do."

"OK, Kyle. I'll talk to you later." Just as I was about to end the call, I heard Kyle scream my name. "What Kyle?" I asked even more irritated than before.

My desire was to return to a deep sleep but, I couldn't seem to get this Negro off my phone. For a split second, I thought of hanging up, acting as if I didn't hear him blaring my name into the receiver, but I realized it would only make him call back.

"Can I come over later?" he asked, softly.

"For what?"

"To talk. I've got this bad feeling something is going on with Dani, and I need you to be my sounding board. I need a rational thinker in my corner right now because my thoughts are all over the place."

In his corner? I'm not his wife. Not even his friend. "And where are your friends—the fellas? You can't chat with them before going out to the club tonight? It's Friday, ya know? Big club night, isn't it?"

"Stop playin', Tori. This is serious. I don't even go to the clubs like that no more. I just need someone to talk to, and I choose you. Are you up for it later this evening?"

Something within told me that if I didn't agree to meeting with Kyle, I'd never get him off my phone. So, I did. "Look, Kyle. I really don't want to be caught in this mess, but if you really need to talk I'll let you come over for a few minutes. Is six o'clock good for you?"

"Perfect. Thanks again, Tori. I'll see you later."

Ugh. Kyle was definitely not incorporated into my plans for the day—not the morning wake-up call, and definitely not the

Friday evening visit. The last thing I wanted was to be in the presence of Kyle, listening to him talk about my nemesis. But, I'd be lying if I said I wasn't curious about what he wanted to discuss. Could there be trouble brewing in the Monroe household? Had Kyle finally regretted his decision to marry my sister? Hmmmmmmmm. I figured I'd have all my questions answered in a few hours. But until then, I'd hibernate under my comforter

Chapter 17

Dani

"Dani . . . Dani . . . Wake up," Zach shrieked, while sternly jolting my arm.

With my head still buried in the plush pillow, I barked, "Stop hittin' me. What's your problem?"

"You've got to get up. It's seven thirty in the morning. I must've fallen asleep last night before waking you. My alarm clock didn't go off this morning and now I'm late for work . . . and you, a married woman, stayed out all night."

"Awww, hell!" I jumped from Zach's bed.

"Aw, hell is right. This is one big mess. Kyle is probably worried to death about you."

"I can only imagine. But, you don't worry about Kyle. I can handle him. He's definitely pissed off, but I think I smooth this over."

"Dani, please come back to reality. This isn't a joke. Kyle is going to skin you alive. This is beyond crazy. We're getting sloppy, Dani. Tori and Kyle are bound to get suspicious. I promised Tori I'd call her when I got home last night and didn't because you were here. You promised Kyle you'd be home by nine last night and didn't come home at all."

Zach was in full drama king mode. He paced around the room, rubbing his temples and arguing with me over spilled milk. What was done was done, and I let him know that.

"You're right. We've been sloppy. But, Kyle will be fine. I'll tell him I drank too much while over to Capri's and couldn't drive home."

"And your reason for not calling him?"

"Because I'm a grown ass woman. You don't seem to understand that. I rule the Monroe household. I wear the pants. You may be afraid of Tori, but I don't fear Kyle. Yeah, it's messed up what I did, but stuff happens. It was a mistake."

"You're killing me with this callous attitude. This has got to stop, and I mean it. I love Tori, and what we're doing is wrong. I'm a minister for God's sake, and I'm caught up in an affair with a married woman. I'm cheating on my fiancée all the while counseling youth at work and preaching to them at church. This is hypocrisy at its finest. And no matter how you feel about Kyle, he's a good man. I have no ill feelings toward the brother. He's been nothing but kind to me and it pains me to shake his hand and smile in his face every time our paths cross. This can't continue. This messy, lustful relationship is bound to get us both in trouble."

"In trouble? In trouble? Are we not adults? There's no sending us to the principal's office. There's no putting us in time-out. Come on, I told you I've got this covered. So, I'm not understanding why you're still walking around in a frenzy about something I can handle."

"It's more than just this. It's everything. I'm sick of it. My conscience can't continue to allow me to be with you. I just can't. I can't." Zach rushed over to the nightstand and grabbed the telephone receiver. Undoubtedly he was calling Tori.

"Shhhhh, don't say a word. Just get dressed," he said.

I gave him the who-you-think-you-talking-to look followed by a long eye roll. He'd want not to speak to me that way because surely I'd make my presence known while he was talking to Tori.

As I slowly and quietly dressed, I listened attentively to his conversation. "Hey, sweetheart."

Another eye roll. No he didn't have the nerve to call her "sweetheart" after lying up with me all night.

"Are you sleeping?" he asked. "Okay, well, I just wanted to apologize for not calling you last night. It completely slipped my mind. It won't happen again." There was a pause.

"Honey? Honey? Are you there? Oh, I thought you hung up. I'll let you get back to sleep, but wanted to know if you wanted to do dinner tonight. With whom? What do you mean it's none of my concern? Stop playing, Tori and just tell me." Zach was getting irritated. He stopped speaking for about thirty seconds. Then he took the phone away from his ear and said, "She hung up on me."

Inwardly, I laughed. "Why?"

"Why do you think? She's pissed at me. I've been slacking lately, and she sees it. She doesn't deserve this. I have no idea why I'm doing this to her. This isn't how a man of God should be conducting himself. We . . . we can't keep doing this. There's too much at stake. I'm feeling like I've got a special place in Hell for me right now."

"That's what your mouth says, Zachary, but you know you don't want to stop dealing with me. You say this all the time and quite frankly it's becoming redundant. Either we're done or we're not, but stop throwing it in my face. You know the chemistry is dynamic between us, and you know you don't come close to feeling the same sparks when you're with Tori. So, stop frontin'. You don't have to marry her. You always have the option of calling off the wedding and remain a single man. I'd even divorce Kyle. That way you don't have to feel all guilty about the happiness and satisfaction you feel when you're with me."

"Call off the wedding? Are you serious? I'm not calling off the wedding. I'm going to marry Tori. I love her. I don't know why you can't seem to get that through your thick skull."

Sarcastically, I retorted, "Ummmmmm, maybe because I'm twisting and turning in your bed more than your fiancée. Ever think of that?"

"And therein lies the problem. When I became a man, I vowed that I'd never do what my father did to my mother. He was unfaithful to her throughout their marriage. For years, my mother cried and prayed about her marriage. As a boy, I saw her pain. I felt her anguish. Behind closed doors, I ached for her, but I never let her see. I had to stay strong for her. Even though she thought I was oblivious to what was going on, I knew everything. I heard the arguments. I saw him with other women. I saw it all, and as a lad, I gave my word that I'd never treat the woman I professed to love in that manner. Now look at me. A clone of my father—a man I loathe and distrust."

I guess Zachary didn't notice how unmoved I was by his little speech. I was all for a man wanting to honor his vows to his wife, but he wasn't married yet nor had this been an issue for the past year. So, the sudden act of morality was baffling to me. "So, what do you really want, Zach? I mean seriously."

"I want you to finish getting dressed, and go home to your husband. Stop all this talk about divorcing him. Work things out with him. Try rebuilding what you have, and let's end this thing between us today. I care about you, but I'm in love with your sister, and she's gonna be my wife. I need to start acting like it. Can you respect that?"

A spirit of rebellion came across me. Slowly unbuttoning the blouse that I had put on moments prior, I seductively said, "I can respect your position. But, the least you can do is give me one more morning of passion before we call it quits. Give me a nice send-off."

"No, Dani. We're done. I'm not doing this any—"

After being with a person intimately for a year or more, you learn what methods to use to get them hot and bothered. Needless to say, I had succeeded in silencing Zachary Ambrose and received my so-called last morning of passion.

Then, it was time to go home to face Kyle, who probably was furious with me.

Chapter 18

Tori

As planned, Kyle was ringing my doorbell at six o'clock on the dot. Surprisingly, I was looking forward to his visit. I wasn't sure if that was because I was dying to hear some dirt about Dani or if I just wanted to be in the presence of a male since I was on the outs with Zach. Nevertheless, I prepared a spaghetti dinner with a garden salad and garlic bread just in case he wanted a bite to eat. Oddly, I also went the extra mile to make sure I was looking flawless. My hair was freshly done, my make-up was unblemished.

Nothing was right about this visit. The fact that Kyle was coming and my preparation for his arrival were all rather outrageous. What the hell was really going on?

"I appreciate you allowing me to come over to speak with you," Kyle said, as he entered my apartment door.

Surprisingly, he leaned in to hug me. Not sure how to take it, I gave him the famous "friend" hug while gently patting him on his back. I have to admit, I was blown away when I got a whiff of his Lacoste cologne. My god. He smelled delicious. And he looked good, too. I was beginning to think his visit was a bad idea.

Focus, Tori, focus, I reminded myself. *This man is not my friend. He's your ex-boyfriend who married your sister. Can't get more trifling than that.* I regained my composure then responded to him. "Have a seat, Kyle. Would you like something to drink or eat?"

"No, thank you," he said looking around my 1,200 square foot apartment. "Tori, I really like your apartment. I've never had the pleasure of coming here, so I didn't know you had such a nice place."

"And before today, what reason would you have to come to my home?"

"Awww, hell. I see you ain't tryna cut a brotha no slack. You aren't gonna be nice to me are you?"

I smiled. "What makes you say that? You're here, aren't you?"

"Yeah, but I can tell by your 'tude that you really don't want me here. Is my assessment correct?"

"Some of what you say is true. I guess the uncertainty of your being here is what has me on edge. I'm not sure we really have anything to discuss. But curiosity is getting the best of me, so that's why you're here. But, please know that if I truly didn't want you here, you wouldn't be."

"I messed you up pretty badly by hooking up with Dani, huh? You're never going to forgive me, are you?"

"How can you fix your lips to ask me such a thing? Sadly, I will probably have to forgive you because I do want to make Heaven my home when I die, but if it weren't for that, I would never, ever forgive you. You hurt me more than any man I've ever known. The pain I felt after finding out you were with Dani was comparable to having open heart surgery without anesthesia. For months, I didn't know if I could overcome the agony caused by this. And it didn't make matters any better when Dani eagerly tormented me about dating you. Do you have any idea . . . I mean any idea, how I felt back then? Do you?" I was livid.

Talking about this with Kyle was probably unhealthy. I was bound to relive that mess all over again. I remember the conversation with Dani just like it happened thirty minutes ago.

I was at work, assisting a group of students with a math assignment when the secretary called to the classroom and informed me I had a telephone call. Instantly, I became nervous because I didn't get phone calls at work. I figured something had happened to Mama or Daddy. When I reached the main office, the secretary told me the caller was holding on line two. I picked up the receiver and nervously greeted the caller. And to my surprise, it was Dani.

"Hey, Sis. Didn't mean to interrupt your lesson." She laughed. "Aw, I'm sorry. You're not a teacher. You don't teach lessons."

I ignored her degrading comments. I still thought something was really wrong. So, I asked, "Is something wrong with Mama or Daddy?"

Again, she chuckled. "No, dear heart. This is not an emergency call. This is more of an informative call."

"Huh?" I was beyond confused.

"Listen. And listen attentively. That man you let go is my man now."

Still baffled, I said, "What are you talkin' about?"

"I forgot I was talking to the uneducated here. Listen, Sister. I am now screwing Kyle. Do you understand me now? He's my man . . . the one you let get away. See what being all high and mighty gets you? Nothing. Absolutely nothing. Peace."

When she hung up, I stood holding the phone to my ear in disbelief. I was stunned. I couldn't fathom why, my own sister, the professional assistant principal, would take time out of her schedule to call me at work to announce she's dating my ex-boyfriend. But although, I was shocked by this revelation, I didn't fully believe Dani. She didn't have a good reputation for being credible. I needed confirmation from Kyle. So, after I struggled to get through the rest of my work day, I rushed home and called him as soon as I closed the door behind me. To my dismay, he hesitantly and apologetically confirmed what Dani said was true. I slammed the phone in his ear and cried my eyes out. I could expect this type of backstabbing from Dani, but never would have guessed that Kyle would be apart of her foolishness, especially knowing our history.

"Kyle you of all people know what I had endured with Dani. You held me many nights as I cried about her treachery. You claimed you were on my side. You claimed to dislike her because of her actions toward me. You claimed you'd curse her out if I ever decided to let you loose and get at her. You claimed you . . . you . . . you . . . you claimed you love me. So, how could you?"

I unexpectedly began weeping. This certainly wasn't in my plans. I never wanted Kyle to see how much he'd hurt me. But, it was too late to mask it now. The tears wouldn't stop.

Wiping the tears from my eyes, Kyle's face bore expressions of guilt and compassion. An unanticipated sorrow came over his face. I could tell he really regretted what he had done. His words to me said it all.

"Tori, baby. If I could take it all back I would. I knew what I had done was horribly wrong. But, I didn't think it would be so hurtful to you because you ended things between us. I thought you didn't care and couldn't care less what I did and who I did it with. Now, I realize my assumption of how you felt was totally wrong. I'm so sorry, Tori. I'm so, sorry baby. I really am. I can only hope that one day you can find it in your heart to forgive me."

His apology seemed heartfelt. He seemed as if he was torn just as much as me. But then I remembered something else was going on with Kyle. He asked to come over to speak with me about something. It was time we got to the real reason behind his visit.

"Kyle," I said with a slight smile. "I do forgive you. At this moment, I forgive you. I didn't think I ever could, but when I look deep into your brown eyes, I can see your sadness for what you've done. But, I can't seem to shake this feeling that your sadness has another meaning, a deeper meaning. What's going on, Kyle?"

Kyle's head hung low. His eyes no longer met mine. It took him a few minutes to speak. I didn't rush him. I allowed him to sit in silence until he felt comfortable opening up to me.

Taking a deep breath, he said, "I think I married the wrong one."

Astonished, I asked, "Whatchu say?"

"I think I married the wrong Prescott girl. I should've fought for you, Tori. I shouldn't have let you leave my life so easily. And I damn sure shouldn't have ever hooked up with your sister. Now, I'm paying a heavy price for marrying the wrong woman, the wrong twin. I had a good thing going with you, Tori, and I messed it up. I thought I could rehash what I had with you with Dani, but I was wrong as two left feet."

Slightly flattered, I said, "Wait. Wait. Wait. Where is all of this coming from? What's going on?"

"I think Dani is messin' around," he spoke delicately as his eyes stayed glued to the floor.

"Really? I asked placing my hand gently on his knee. "What makes you think that?"

"Tori, I'm a man. I know the games *we* play. I know the games I've played, and I know the games my male friends play. She's displaying all the classic signs of cheating."

"Classic signs? What signs?"

"Hmm, where shall I began? Let's see, there is the sad fact that she's not having sex with me, she's rarely home, and she can't use the excuse of working late since she hasn't been to work since the baby's death. When she is at home, she's holed up in the bedroom, claiming she needs to be alone or she'll stage petty arguments to have a reason to storm out the house. I've discovered she's been visiting chat rooms and has signed up for Yahoo! Messenger, so she's chatting with someone online, and to put the icing on the cake, she didn't come home last night. So, what else am I supposed to think?"

"Man, Kyle, you're right. This doesn't sound good. I can't believe she's been doing all of this. When did it start?"

"Shortly after she returned home from the hospital. Before that, she had some late nights out, but she attributed those to work. Some of that I can vouch for because assistant principals don't have a set schedule. She could be at work as late at eight at night. But, I still believe something was going on back then. I was just oblivious to it."

I really didn't know what to say to Kyle. My gut told me he was right about Dani. Because I know her to be self-centered and insensitive to other people's feelings, it wasn't far fetched for me to believe that she was out in the streets mimicking the behaviors of a harlot. But, I didn't want to add to Kyle's uneasy feelings by confirming what he believed to be true. I just said the only thing I knew to say next.

"Kyle, I'm sorry to hear you've been dealing with this. I feel for you. I'm speechless. And I don't know how I can help."

"I'm not here to ask you for help. I just wanted someone to talk to because I'm thinking of doing something to catch Dani in her mess."

With raised eyebrows, I looked at him sideways. "What in the world are you talking about? Please, Kyle don't do anything crazy."

"Tori, if I tell you, you have to promise to keep this between us. If I find out you told your parents, Zach, Denise or any of those church folks, I'm gonna be pissed. I'm trusting you with this info and only you."

"I won't say anything, as long as it's nothing illegal. If you're planning to commit a crime of some sort, then I don't even wanna know." I couldn't believe I was so eager to listen to Kyle's scheme. I guess a part of me secretly wanted him to get the goods on Dani.

Kyle grinned. "I ain't committing no crimes. I'm just gonna get to the bottom of what's going on."

"So, what are you planning to do?" I asked a little too eagerly.

"Aiight, here's the plan."

I sat dumfounded as I listened to Kyle's plans to catch Dani doing the unthinkable. He hadn't set everything into motion, but he had what he needed to get things going. I continually told him it wasn't a good idea, but it was hard getting through to him. He was a man on a mission. Nothing or no one could've changed his mind. It was time for Dani to fall and maybe Kyle would be the perfect person to bring her down. Although, he'd hurt me deeply, something in me hated seeing him in pain. So, I wrapped my arms around him, sympathetically kissed his cheek and held him tightly in my arms. Before he left, I told him I was in support of his "Expose the Cheater" operation. Sad shame, I was enjoying this so much.

Chapter 19

Dani

I had finally made my way home by late morning, after fighting the morning rush hour traffic. Kyle wasn't home. I let out a deep sigh of relief. He must've been at work. I paused in the living room for a brief moment, just shaking my head at my actions. I couldn't believe I had stayed out all night. Even *I* realized there was no excuse for this type of behavior.

I hadn't even called Kyle. The least I could've done was notified him that I was still alive via e-mail, text message, something, but I did nothing. Because of this, I decided to just take whatever Kyle was going to say—within reason. I wasn't going to fight or argue with him. I really didn't have a leg to stand on. As hard as it was to admit, I was wrong.

I had braced myself for the confrontation that would ensue between Kyle and me when I saw him. I practiced all afternoon what I'd say. I had my speech fully memorized and I was prepared. However, Kyle still wasn't home. It was getting late into the evening hours. I was beginning to wonder if he was planning to stay out all night—one of those payback moves.

I thought about calling Zach, but before I left him, he made it clear that things between us were over. Although, I didn't believe him for a second, I thought giving him some space and time to miss me would assist with having me back in his arms.

Shortly after 8 P.M., I had taken a long, hot bath. The bath was soothing to my body, but not my mind. Kyle still hadn't walked through the door. I lay across my bed and began channel surfing. I was beginning to worry. What nerve, right? This was unlike him. He was such a sweet guy, dedicated to our marriage, catered to me and my every need, so for him to stay out so late was definitely strange.

I jumped when I heard the front door slam. First, I was relieved that Kyle was fine. But, I knew his arrival meant it was time for combat. I had prepared myself to just take Kyle's tongue-lashing. There was no need in getting into an argument with him and possibly blurting out something I'd regret about my affair with Zach, or risk having a look of guilt sprawled across my face. I'd planned to let Kyle win this argument—but only because I'd organized a forfeit.

When Kyle entered the bedroom door, I could see fury in his eyes. This was a look I'd never seen Kyle wear. He almost looked possessed.

"Where the hell have you been?" he bellowed.

I took a deep breath. *Here we go*, I thought. *Keep your cool, Dani. Let him be the victor this once*, I reminded myself.

"Hi, Kyle." I gave a weak smile.

"I don't wanna hear nothing from you but an explanation. So, save the greetings."

"Kyle, I know you're angry. You have every right to be. I'm sorry I didn't call last night. I was wrong. I promise it won't happen again."

I laughed inside. I was sure Kyle wasn't used to me giving in this easily. I knew he was all set for me to give him mad attitude. I could tell by the way his facial expression changed that I had shocked him.

"I'm glad you realize you're wrong, but that still doesn't answer my question. Where were you, Dani?"

"With Capri. Last night I was at her house, had too many drinks and fell asleep. When I woke up, it was daylight."

"So, it's just that simple. With Capri, drank too much, fell asleep," he mimicked. "Do you really expect me to believe that?"

"Call Capri. She'll confirm it."

"You must think I'm an idiot, right? You must not be aware that I know how to play games, too. You must not know 'bout me, for real. Come on. Come better than the 'call Capri' line. I ain't falling for it."

"Why not?"

"Ummmmmm, because I know how this game works, Dani. You've already talked to Capri and asked her to cover for you. I'm not stupid, and I *am* a man."

"Well, honey, I don't know what else to say. I was with Capri and no where else. I'm sorry you don't believe me, but it's true."

"Cut your bullshit. I don't believe you. You're lying to me, and I know it."

I was starting to get a bit testy. I had apologized and admitted my wrong doing. What else did he want? "Kyle, there is no need to belabor the point. I was totally out of line. I'll say it fifty more times if you want me to. It won't happen again. What else can I say?"

"You can tell me what man's bed you were in last night?"

"What?" I snapped. "What the hell are you talking about?"

Ok. I felt like I was about to lose my cool. This is where I had to regain my composure. Once the allegations started, I knew I'd get in a heated debate with Kyle trying to defend myself. This was when I knew I'd make the mistake of outing myself. So, I remained calm.

"Dani, all the signs are there. You are never here, we don't have sex, there is no affection, no quality time, no nothing. So, if you're not giving it up to me, your husband, then who are you giving it up to?"

"You're mistaken, Kyle. I'm not seeing another man. I love you," I said innocently. I did love Kyle. I just wasn't madly in love with him. I saw him as an opportunity to get back at Tori and to father my first born. I didn't think I'd ever have real feelings for him, but I developed them over time.

"You love me? You love me?" He laughed. "Get outta here with that shit. You don't love me. You never have. I was just a pawn to you. You just used me to hurt Tori and because I was blinded by a big butt and a smile, I fell for it. I thought being with you would rekindle the same loving feelings I had for Tori. I was totally wrong about that. If only I knew then what I know now . . ."

"How dare you, Kyle Monroe. How dare you say those things to me? I didn't use you. I genuinely liked you when we started dating and loved you when I married you," I lied. "And what do you mean you only fell for me because you wanted what you had with Tori." That comment had fire shooting through my veins.

"It meant just what I said. I had something good with Tori and didn't realize it until she broke things off with me. Then when you pursued me, I just knew that I'd get that same warm and fuzzy feeling from you, her twin sister. Sadly, that dream proved to be erroneous. What I got was great pleasure in the bedroom, which made me think I was getting something more from you, like a stronger bond. Now I realize it was lust, not love."

"Kyle," I screamed. "Stop it." He was really hurting my feelings. I mean, to compare me to Tori was the worst feeling ever. I began to feel tears form in the back of my eyes. This conversation was really taking a turn for the worse.

"Stop what? You can't handle the truth? You think I'm some soft dude, right? All in the name of love or what I thought was love. I've let you run things around here long enough. I've let you call all the shots. I've let you dictate our wedding, the plans for the baby, the bills, the living arrangement, everything. And now I'm fed up. I don't need you, Dani, for nothing. I can walk out that front door right now and never, ever look back because I don't need you."

The tears that formed had now fallen down my cheeks. Kyle had never spoken to me so harsh. Hell, I couldn't think of any man ever speaking to me like Kyle did. I was always treated with respect. Men always told me how much I was needed, how they didn't want to live without me, how much they loved me, how beautiful I was, and every other tender, loving comment that soothed a woman's soul. But, now, my husband was telling me he didn't need me. This was more hurtful than anyone could ever imagine. And because all this was new to me, I really didn't know how to handle it. My first reaction was to say, "get to steppin" because I surely could handle my own. But, the competitor in me kept whispering things in my ear like, *You can't let Kyle go. If he leaves, Tori will win. She'll be elated. She'll rejoice in your failed marriage. Besides, you can't let him end the marriage. It's only over when you say it's over.*

"Kyle, you're saying some very hurtful things. There's no need for you to walk out the door. We're going through a rough patch. We can get through this. It sounds like we have some issues that we both need to get out on the table, and I'm willing to do that. You just have to be open to giving us a chance."

"Give us a chance? Why? You don't love me, Dani. You haven't acted like my wife since our wedding day. So, why keep up this façade?"

"Kyle, please don't do this," I said, walking over toward him. I put my arms around him and whispered, "We can make this work. I promise to be a better wife." Then I gave him a soft peck on his lips. Then another. And another. With each kiss, I felt Kyle giving in.

Softly, he said, "Dani, I love you. I want this to work, but I'm not your puppet, your slave, or your door mat. You are gonna have to respect me or I'm out. Plain and simple."

"I'll work on it, Kyle. I promise," I said then kissed him passionately.

I wanted all of this to go away. The argument made me realize a few things about myself and Kyle as well. Kyle was a smart man and a good man. For some reason, I took his kindness for weakness. Instead of walking over him, I wondered how it would be to just respect him as my husband. Wasn't it time I stopped playing games? Wasn't it time I stopped messing around with Tori's or someone else's man? Wasn't it time to stop being the jump-off, the side chick, the mistress? Didn't I deserve better than second best? Many women would love to have a man like Kyle by their side, and I was abusing it.

It was at that moment I realized I needed to reevaluate my life because if I didn't, I may just find myself alone. With my head buried in his shoulder, I said, "Kyle, I'm sorry. I hope we can move past this."

Kyle wrapped his arms around me and said, "We'll see, Dani. We'll see."

Chapter 20

June 2009
Tori

After meeting with Kyle, my thoughts were consumed with him and his ultimate plan to find the goods on Dani. I realized it weighed on me far more than it should have. It wasn't my life thus it wasn't my concern. I wished Kyle all the best, but I had to move on with planning my future with my fiancé.

A week later, I made dinner plans with Zach and my parents hoping to get my mind off Kyle and Dani's problems and back on my upcoming nuptials.

"Tori and Zach, I must say that was a wonderful meal. I'm full as a tick," Daddy said, rubbing his stomach.

Zach and I had taken Mommy and Daddy out to their favorite soul food restaurant, Sampson's. They had just stuffed themselves silly with fried chicken, collard greens, macaroni and cheese and hot buttered rolls. Daddy had pushed his chair back from the table and gently rubbed his stomach in circular motions.

"Oh, Mr. Prescott, it was our pleasure," Zach said. "After all you and the Mrs. have done to assist us with wedding preparations, it's the least we can do."

Chiming in, Mommy said, "Speaking of the wedding, you only have about three weeks to go. I know the arrangements are all in order, but what about the house hunting. How's that going?"

"Mommy, we're still working with our realtor. We have settled on a nice, quiet neighborhood in the Pikesville area. It's just that with our hectic schedules, we haven't really had time to go see any of the houses up for sale."

"What y'all waitin' for? Y'all better hop on it. You'll be married before you know it. And where will you live?"

"Oh, Mommy. We've got time. It's not like we'll be homeless. We've already discussed it. If we haven't settled on a house before the wedding, we'll live in my apartment until—" I lost my train of thought when my cell phone rang. I quickly pulled it from my purse and the caller ID revealed Kyle's number. I ignored it and placed it back in my bag. "Sorry, y'all. Anyway, we'll live in my apartment until we find our dream home," I said, looking into Zach's charming eyes. I was getting so excited about our impending nuptials that I didn't know if I'd be able to compose myself. More and more the thought of becoming Mrs. Zachary Ambrose gave me such an extraordinary feeling, more than I could ever put into words.

Mommy asked, "So, how is the marriage counseling going?"

"It's going well," Zach answered.

"Yeah, Ma. I've really enjoyed the first two sessions we've had with Pastor Brice."

"What have you enjoyed thus far?" Daddy inquired.

"Well, during the first two sessions, we delved into each of our expectations of marriage, what we thought of ourselves and each other, appreciating each other's differences, our families, communication and financial management. During our last session, we are expected to discuss conflict resolution, balancing private time together and experiencing intimacy within marriage."

"Ah, that last one, is quite important, kiddo," Daddy said, teasingly.

"Norm," Mommy said as she playfully hit him on the arm.

"What? I'm just telling her like it is. Intimacy within a marriage is extremely important, and I ain't just talking about sex. Where's your mind at, woman? There's more to intimacy than doing the do. You don't know that by now? We've only been married ninety-nine years."

We all fell into laugher. Daddy was cutting up. He was trying to save himself, but because he was a man, I knew he was talking about sex, too.

Again, our dinner conversation was interrupted by the sound of my cell phone chiming. This time it was the text indicator. I knew it was Kyle.

"Honey, who's trying so hard to reach you?" Zach questioned.

"I don't know. Mommy is here with me, and she's the only one who blows up my cell phone all day and night."

"Watch it, girl," Mommy jokingly snapped.

I scrolled through to check the message and just as I predicted it was Kyle. The message read: I AM HIRING A P.I. TOMORROW. KYLE.

Stunned by his message, my jaws dropped. Kyle wasn't playing. It seemed as if the battle lines had been drawn and he was about to stir up some serious conflict. He must've felt something deep within his core to go to this extreme to have Dani followed—something equivalent to if not stronger than women's intuition.

"What's wrong, Tori? Who was that? Is everything okay?" Zach asked

"Yeah, sweetie, you look like you've seen a ghost," Mommy added.

With a nervous smiled, I responded, "Oh, that was Denise. Everything is fine. She just wants me to call her when I get home. It seems there's something important she has to tell me."

"Are you sure, honey?" Zach asked.

"Yes, I'm sure. I just hope everything is all right with her, that's all. But, hey, is anybody up for dessert. I have a taste for some strawberry cheesecake." This was my weak attempt to deflect the conversation away from me, the text message and the lie I had just told. It worked.

"I think I'll have a slice of apple pie," Daddy said.

"Norm, you don't need another thing to eat."

"Says, who?" Daddy asked with one eyebrow raised.

"Says me."

Ignoring Mommy, Daddy said, "Zach, let me give you a piece of advice I know Pastor Brice won't tell you during counseling. Don't let this woman," he said pointing to me, "tell you what you can and cannot eat."

Zach laughed. I just shook my head at him.

"I'm serious, Zachary. Tori's my daughter, and I love her dearly, but don't let her tell you what to put in your stomach." He paused. "Tori, if this man wants a bucket of buffalo wings with blue cheese dip, followed by a big hunk of chocolate cake. Let 'em. If he decides to chow down on a big ole greasy cheese steak sub coupled with an order of fries, let 'em. Don't be tryin' to make him no chicken Caesar salad if he doesn't want that."

I was literally in tears from laughter. Daddy was breaking it down, sharing his "Norm-isms" and Zach seemed to love every minute of it. Mommy, on the other hand, looked at him as if he was absolutely crazy, but I could tell she was holding back her laughter. No matter how silly Daddy acted, I could tell Mommy was in love with her husband.

We listened as Daddy continued with his marital rules. "Oh, yeah and there's something else you need to learn and quickly. Make note of this because it's important. Men are satisfied with three things in a marriage."

"And what are those three things, Daddy?"

"Minimal chatter, good food, and good...well, you know. It goes back to the intimacy thing we talked about earlier."

Daddy was on a roll. If I hadn't known better, I would've thought he had a few drinks or something. I appreciated his humor, though. It felt good to laugh. It felt good that things were back on track with Zach. It felt good to be in the midst of my parents without having to share the time with Dani. It was wonderful not having to hear her name mentioned one time during the entire dinner. Prayerfully, this was a sign of things to come—a great beginning with my new husband—free from Dani and her drama. That would be the biggest blessing and the best wedding present ever.

Just as I was basking in the moment, my cell phone chimed for a third time. Another text message—from Kyle. My eyes hurriedly read the words displays on my cell phone's screen. My heart sank. Kyle second message only confirmed that he was out for blood—Dani's blood.

Chapter 21

Dani

Making things work with Kyle hadn't been easy. I had been striving hard to make our marriage work—to become a better wife. At times, I felt pretty genuine in my efforts, and other times, I felt as if I was just going through the motions. Preparing home-cooked meals, having the house sparkling clean when Kyle returned home from work and lounging around with him in our TV room were pretty much authentic. I enjoyed doing those things for him, and he seemed receptive of my attempts to better our relationship.

But, in the bedroom is where I struggled. Each time I lay with Kyle, my thoughts were always on Zach. Kyle just couldn't do for me what Zach could intimately. He didn't make me feel as special. He didn't make me feel as if making love to me was something he longed for. Zach had this exceptional way of making me feel as if he had desired me for a lifetime. That feeling was something I missed deeply and yearned for it time and time again. But, I was an actress in the bedroom, I don't think Kyle noticed—at least I hoped he didn't.

In the midst of trying to improve my marriage, I still couldn't dissolve the constant thoughts of Zach. It was actually disconcerting because it seemed as if he was true to his word when he said he was done with me. I hadn't heard from him since the day I accidentally spent the night at his place. I sent him an email and received no response. I sent him a text message and again, no response. I was holding off on calling him because I was fearful of the reaction I'd get if he answered. His ignoring my attempts to contact him coupled with what he said the last time I saw him, made it absolutely clear as to where we stood, but I still fought to get him out my system. Zach was almost like a drug, and I was definitely detoxifying. Not a good feeling at all.

Just as I was finishing up dinner, Kyle walked through the door. I turned to him. "Hey, babe. How was your day?" I asked.

"All right," he said in somewhat of a somber tone.

"What's wrong with you?"

"Nothing," he snapped.

Wanting to pry further, I didn't. I was trying to keep the peace in the Monroe household. I'd just let him wallow in the nasty attitude by himself. "Dinner is ready. You can eat when you get ready."

"I'm not eating. I'm headed back out."

"Back out? Where are you going?"

"I'm going to Happy Hour with Foster, Daniel and Eric."

"Foster? Daniel? Eric? I haven't heard those names in months."

"Yeah, that's the point. Because I was so wrapped up into you, I put my boys on the back burner, but that's all about to end. I'm hanging out with my friends tonight. Sorry, you wasted time cooking. Maybe I'll eat it tomorrow."

"Kyle, you could've told me you weren't going to be here. I wouldn't have bothered to even prepare dinner. That's so inconsiderate of you."

"Dani, please. Let's not even talk about inconsideration." He chuckled. "You don't even want to go there."

"You know what, Kyle?" I paused to gather my thoughts because I was quite perturbed. "Go out, have your fun and make sure you come back with a better attitude. I'm sick of you acting like you love me and want to work things out one minute and the next, you're walking around like you hate me. I'm fed-up with this wishy-washy attitude."

He laughed again. "Like I said: I'm not going there with you today. I hear a bottle of Cognac calling my name. I'm out."

"Ugggggggggggggggggggggggggh," I screamed, letting out some heat.

I had been trying and trying and trying with Kyle, but if he thought for one second I was going to sit back and let him walk all over me, he had better think again. Did he not know who I was? Did he not know what I was capable of? Did he not know that I really didn't need him and was only with him to save face? Did he not know that the last exchange was the end of me trying to be the "good wife?" I was too through. He could stick a fork in me because I was well done.

After taking a few moments to calm down, I decided that I had been put off and ignored long enough. I needed to speak with Zach. I needed to see him. I needed to feel his lips pressed against mine. I needed my Zach fix, and I wasn't taking "no" for an answer.

Slowly, I dialed his number. The phone rang once . . .

twice . . . a third time . . . and a fourth. I was all prepared to leave a seductively sweet message until he answered. "Hey, baby. It's me, Dani."

Chapter 22

Tori

"Hurry up and get in here," I barked, yanking Kyle by his sleeve. He had called twenty-minutes prior to showing up at my front door. As much as I wanted no parts of this mess with Kyle and Dani, I felt as if I kept allowing Kyle to pull me deeper and deeper into it. I should've been ashamed, but I wasn't. "What in the world is wrong with you?"

He laughed. "What do you mean? I'm good."

"No you're not, Kyle. And stop laughing. This mess is craaaaaaaaaazy. I almost died when I got that text from you last night. You knew I was out with my parents and Zach at the time. I couldn't believe you actually went through with the plan of hiring a P.I. When I read the text, my whole demeanor changed, and it was noticeable. They questioned me as to what was wrong, but I made up a story about something going on with Denise. You got me lying to my parents and fiancé, man. What in the world have you gotten me into?"

Holding up his hands, Kyle said, "Slow down. Slow down. I haven't gotten you into anything. I just put you down with my plan. You have nothing to do with this. I just wanted you to know. It's my idea. It's my money paying for the service, and it's my wife that I believe is hiding something. This really has nothing to do with you."

"Oh, please, Kyle. If that's the case, then why did you tell me? You could've kept this info to yourself."

"Look, sweetheart," Kyle spoke.

I shot him a look. "'Sweetheart?' 'Sweetheart?' I ain't your 'sweetheart.'"

"Whatever, Tori. You'll always be my sweetheart. You can fight it all day and night for the rest of your life, but I know you still love me."

Truth be told, Kyle was right. I didn't have deep, take-a-bullet type of love for him, but I did love him. I knew he would always have a special place in my heart, but that wasn't something I could ever admit to him. Jokingly, I said, "Kyle, please. Get over yourself. I love Zach, and that's it."

"OK. If you say so. Anyway, back to the topic, *sweetheart*. Right now, you're all I've got. I don't want you to participate in any of this. I just need you to be a listening ear. That's it. You know better than anybody what life with Dani is like, so I feel that we share something in this. Nobody else can relate. It's kind of like you're my sounding board."

"Again, I ask, where are your friends?"

"Where do you think I got the P.I. suggestions from? My boy, Daniel's dad is a former law enforcement agent who now is a private investigator. I've already met with him and got the ball rolling."

"What do you mean, you've 'got the ball rolling?'"

After I asked, I realized I shouldn't have. The less I knew about the P.I. stuff the better. I could see it clearly—Dani spinning it so that everybody would believe I put Kyle up to hiring an investigator. But it was too late to retract my question. Kyle was eager to share everything with me. As I sat in my kitchen listening to all the details, I couldn't help but think this wasn't what marriage should be about. When one spouse has to stoop to the levels of spending money to hire someone to follow around their mate, something was terribly wrong.

I began to think about my upcoming marriage to Zach and how I really appreciated that we had God in our lives. Having God in the center of a marriage was key. Clearly this was an element that Kyle and Dani didn't have in their union. Although he stabbed me in the back, my heart went out to Kyle. I could see the suffering in his face. I never would've wished this on him— never.

I continued listening to Kyle rambling on about the investiga- tion. He was extremely wound up as he gave me all the details. "Yeah, so it's gonna be like the TV show, *Cheaters*. Dude is gonna be watchin' her every move. I'm talking 'bout taking pictures and everything. She better hope she's walking the straight and narrow 'cause if not, I'm gonna dig in that ass."

"Oh Kyle. Calm down. I'm pretty sure this won't be an episode of *Cheaters*. Besides, why waste the money on an investigation. Just confront her."

Kyle seemed to be getting a little ticked with me. Testily he said, "Confront her? Confront her? I already did. I told her of my suspicions. She denied messing around with another man. Besides, what would you expect her to say, 'Yes, Kyle. I'm cheating.' Please . . . she'll never admit it. Hell, I wouldn't."

"I'll say it again, Kyle. I don't like it—not one bit."

"What is it you don't like, Tori?" Kyle spat.

"I don't like . . . I don't like the fact that I'm not fighting you harder to stop this. I'm ashamed to admit that there's a part of me that wants to see Dani fall. After all she's put me through, I'd love to once and for all see her get what's coming to her. She's been the worst sister ever and I want her to reap every evil, rotten, nasty deed she's ever done to me."

Kyle smiled. "I knew you was frontin' the whole time. You want me to bring her down, dontcha?"

I held my head in shame. Kyle's statement was full of truth.

"You don't have to answer. I know you want me to and believe me when I say, it's already done. Money has been paid and the investigation will be starting. So sit back and enjoy the ride. In the end, your hands won't be dirty in this. It was my doing—all me."

I sighed. Kyle and I had the devil directing our paths and I felt convicted to pray. Hoping that God would change our hearts, I said, "Kyle, let's pray. We are acting like some real demons up in here."

"Pray for what? Like, I said, it's already done."

"Shut up." I ordered. "Now, give me your hands. We're going to pray, if for nothing else, peace of mind and that our hearts will not be filled with revenge."

Hesitantly, Kyle reached his arms across my wooden, round kitchen table and placed his hands in mine. I wrapped my hands tightly around his. For a split second, I felt a tingle inside as I hadn't held his hands in years. Although, he had big, manly hands, they were as soft as a newborn baby's.

After collecting myself and remembering my purpose, I began to speak to God. I humbly asked God to take away the revenge that engulfed our minds and to give Kyle the peace he yearned for in his marriage and in his home. I asked God to reveal to us another method of dealing with this situation and to lead us into righteousness and not on the path of wickedness. This was one time, I surely hoped God's answered prayers swiftly because Kyle and I both needed it.

"Amen." Kyle grinned. "Girl, you still got it. I felt that one. Thank you."

"You're welcome. Now give me my hands back," I teased.

"Tori, I hope God hears your prayer—I really do. I will gladly shut down this investigation, but until I can shake this feeling of uneasiness in the pit of my stomach, which I suffer with daily, I can't. Now, if God comes to me and tells me directly to call it off, I will. Until then, my P.I. will be keeping an eye on Mrs. Monroe."

Shaking my head, I responded, "I'm sorry it's gone this far. My heart aches for you, Kyle. I wish I could do more to help."

"Hey, I'm gonna be fine. I'm not blameless in all of this, ya know? Had I fought harder to be with you, I never would've hooked up with Dani. Had I not gotten caught up in a physical relationship with Dani, I probably wouldn't be here now. So, it's all good. I hurt you, and now she's hurting me. It's called karma," he said as he stared at the floor.

"Pick your head up, boy. You're gonna get through this."

"I know. But do you know what would make me feel a lot better?"

"What?"

"If I could kiss your soft, tender lips for old time's sake," he slyly mouthed.

"OK, Kyle. It's time for you to go." I quickly ushered him to the door. There wasn't gonna be no kissing up in here.

"Alright. Alright. You don't have to rush me out. I was just playing."

"Yeah, right."

"Okay, maybe I lied. I wasn't playing."

Before, I had a moment to protest, Kyle leaned in toward me and gently placed his lips against mine. I was shocked. The tingling instantly returned. Why wasn't I pulling away? Why wasn't I protesting this? Then as quickly as he had stolen that kiss, he disappeared but not before saying goodbye.

"Thanks, Tori. Bye." And with that he was gone.

I closed to the door after Kyle's departure and smiled. What was I smiling about? Another man had just kissed me. Wasn't I engaged to someone else? Wasn't I supposed to be angry? Something wasn't quite right with my reaction. And because of this, I quickly ran to my bedroom to have another talk with Jesus. A sister needed to engage in some serious prayer.

Chapter 23

Dani

"Soooooooooooooo, what's up with you and Kyle?" Capri spoke softly.

We were having lunch at Mo's Seafood Restaurant. I had invited Capri out to lunch before she departed for vacation in London, England. It had always been a dream of hers to travel to London, and after many years of wanting to take the trip, she was on her way.

Many wondered how Capri could ever be friends with me. It was like Cinderella having a bond with one of her evil stepsisters. But, what people didn't know was Capri had been there since childhood. She had seen the pain I endured. She saw the many nights I cried because I was hurt. She was there when my so-called sister belittled and tormented me. She knew my struggles—she lived them with me. So, she knew my heart and knew I wasn't the witch that everyone made me out to be.

"Forget Kyle," I snapped.

With her eyebrows raised, she asked, "What did you say?"

"I said, 'forget Kyle.'"

"No, Dani. I thought you all were working on your marriage. You had been doing so well. What happened?"

"I just can't do it, Capri. I can't. I can't keep putting up this façade. I love Kyle. I really do, but he doesn't fulfill my needs."

"What needs? Sex?"

"You got it."

"Dani. You do know there's more to a marriage than sex. What about all the good Kyle has done for you? Let me break it down for you. You want for nothing. That man pays your mortgage, all the household bills, keeps you laced in diamonds, and you have a wardrobe that looks like everything was purchased on Rodeo Drive in Beverly Hills." Capri paused. "Oh let's put the material stuff to the side and list all the times, he's by your side when you're depressed or how he constantly tip toes around you to keep your anxiety levels low. Or how he's basically thrown his friends to the curb to be with you . You've never had a man like, Kyle. Ever. And you need to realize that he's a damn good man, Dani. I know this and more importantly, you know it. So, stop fakin' like you don't. Sex isn't everything!"

Carpi was right. Everything she said about Kyle was true, but even with all of his wonderful qualities, he still didn't measure up to Zach in the bedroom.

"Sex may not be the most important thing in a marriage for some, but it's number one on my list. Besides, I've finally realized that my heart is with Zach."

Capri gasped. "Huh? Your heart is with Zach? When did this happen? I thought you were just bed buddies. Now, you're telling me you have feelings for him?"

"Time away from him has made me realized that I care more for him than I was willing to admit. I adore Zach. I really do."

"You do realize he's your sister's fiancé, right?"

"Of course, I do. That's what makes this whole thing so wrong. Zach and I belong together. There are genuine feelings between us."

"But, he's Tori's fiancé. What don't you understand about that? Must all your men be a man that had or has a relationship with your sister?"

This was the nice-nasty side of Capri brewing. I could tell she was about to let me have it. Capri wasn't the type of friend to tell me what I wanted to hear—she'd tell me the hard, cold, ugly truth. I braced myself for it because I could sense a lecture coming.

"I know it's baffling. The Kyle thing was strictly revenge. The relationship with Zach started out as revenge, but grew into something more. I had no idea I'd fall for him, Capri. I know we can't ever be a couple, but I'm not ready to fully give him up. I'm so caught up with him that I'm willing to be his mistress—that is, until he comes to his senses."

Capri sat shaking her head at me. I could tell she was disgusted. "I can't believe my ears. Where is my friend, Dani? What have you done with her? I can't possibly be talking to my intelligent, educated, successful friend right now. This must be a clone sitting before me."

"I know it's crazy. I can't believe I'm feeling like this, but it's the truth. I'd be lying to you if I said anything different."

"But, Dani. Why would you ever settle for being someone's mistress? You and I both know you're better than that. Come on, now."

"You're right, but I need Zach in my life. I just need him."

Capri continued to look at me as if I were demon-possessed.

She tried forcefully to get me to see the error of my ways. She made great attempts to help me change my mind about Zach, but to no avail. I had made up my mind that Zach was going to be a part of my life, and I didn't care who disapproved.

After lunch, I wished Capri safe travels. I could tell the enthusiasm about her trip had dwindled a bit after our lunch conversation. Hopefully, once she started hob-knobbing with the English, she'd forget all about me and my issues.

As we departed, a text came through. The message read, "I.H." That was code for, "I'm home."

As soon as Zachary opened his front door, dressed only in his boxer shorts, I immediately began kissing him. Surprisingly, he didn't resist. He was just as much into the kiss, if not more than I was. I hadn't made it inside his apartment completely before he started to undress me. Feeling a bit uneasy about being exposed with the door open, I pulled away from our lip-lock. "Baby, I know you're happy to see me, but shouldn't we close the door first? Wouldn't want the nosey neighbors to see us."

Without saying a word, Zach hurriedly closed the door. He turned to me, eyeing me seductively. He slowly licked his lips, and then without notice, he swept me off my feet and took me to the bedroom. Immediately Kelly Prices' song, "Take Me to a Dream" popped into my head. I knew before we even hit the bedroom that this man was about to fulfill all my fantasies, and I could hardly wait.

With my head gently resting on Zach chest, I whispered, "Thank you."

"For what?" he asked.

"For—for this. My body needed this. I've missed you."

"Same here. I've missed you as well. I didn't realize I was so addicted to you, girl. I had no idea."

I grinned. "Well, what can I say? It's hard to pass on this good thang."

"You ain't lying." He agreed.

"You sure you still wanna walk down that aisle in a couple weeks?"

"Yeah, I'm sure. I have to. I know it may seem twisted, but I do love Tori. I just think that her celibacy has been our biggest problem in our relationship. I've had my needs, and unfortunately, she wasn't able to fulfill them. Not justifying my actions because I know this is horribly wrong, but a man has needs."

"So, what happened to you saying it was over between us? When you weren't responding to my email and text messages, I really thought it was over. I was feeling a bit perturbed about being ignored."

"That was my attempt to fool myself into believing I could cut you off. I've since discovered that it's going to take a supernatural God to help me with this. I'm so hooked on you that I can't see me leaving you at this point. But, after Tori and I are married, things will change—drastically."

"I understand. As long as you're in my life, I'm fine with following the rules. Just as long as you're in my life."

Zach smiled slightly. I could tell he was struggling with marrying Tori. Even though he'd never admit it, I think he wished he could back out of it. I think the pressure from Pastor Brice of wanting the youth pastor married might have had a lot to do with Zach's decision. Of course, this is pure speculation, but that's what I firmly believed.

Realizing that it was getting late, I regrettably told Zach I had to leave. I had been with Zach all afternoon and evening. As much as I wanted to lie in his arms all night, I couldn't risk Kyle breaking my neck for walking in the house after midnight.

"Are you gonna walk me to the car?"

"Sure."

We exited Zach's apartment walking hand in hand. He seemed almost sad that I was leaving—a far cry different than the last time I was at his place. He all but physically put me out that day. But, this day was different.

"Send me a text when you get home. Be discreet. I don't want you and Kyle arguing tonight. You've got to keep a level head. We've made our agreement. I ain't going nowhere, so with that knowledge you should at least be cordial to Kyle—at least try to make home as happy as you can. Okay?"

"OK, Zach. I got it."

Before pulling off, Zach leaned into the car and gave me several quick pecks all over my face. First my forehead, then left cheek, right cheek, tip of my nose but the pecks stopped when he reached my lips. This was a sweet, adoring send-off kiss.

Before pulling off, I mouthed, "Love you, Zachary Ambrose."

He responded, "Much love, sweetheart."

Chapter 24

Tori

Pastor Brice gave off such a warm smile as he sat across from Zach and me. We were in his office wrapping up our last counseling session, ten days shy of the wedding date. He seemed pleased at the progress we had made during counseling. Pastor Brice had given us homework each time he met with us, and we were expected to complete the assignments as well as be prepared to discuss the information at the next session. It seems that Zach and I had passed with flying colors.

Pre-marital counseling with Pastor Brice was quite informative. In three sessions, I learned more about being a wife than I could've ever imagined. For instance, I didn't know withholding sex was a sin. This discussion came about as we discussed intimacy within a marriage. Shocker. But, I was quite confident, this was one sin, I would have no problems avoiding. Zach had been patient with me wanting to remain celibate. Although there were times when we were moments away from crossing the line, we gathered ourselves. Because we were trying to live holy lives, we knew we couldn't put ourselves in compromising situations. We agreed no sex before marriage. It was hard, but we stuck to our commitment. However, on the wedding night, best believe, I was going to give him every ounce of loving I could muster.

I quickly directed my attention back to Pastor Brice and off of sex. How highly inappropriate of me to sit in front of the Pastor thinking about getting it on with Zach.

"All right, kiddos, one last thing before we end this," Pastor Brice said. "Let's talk about conflict resolution." He paused. "You do know that every marriage has its share of energized discussions. Every couple's marriage is tested. Nothing about marriage is easy. It's like having another full-time job. So, let's discuss how you plan to handle those heated little moments when they occur."

"Well, Pastor," Zach spoke, "I think when conflict arises, we should immediately pray."

"That sounds wonderful and logical Zach. The problem is that in the middle of heated battle, while one should stop to pray, one rarely does."

"What about you, Tori? What do you think?"

"I'm not sure I have the answers. I've been known to be pretty quick tempered. I would hope that when the moment of conflict arises we could talk to each other civilly and talk *to* as oppose to *at* one another."

"Those are some good strategies. But, let me give you some key points to dealing with this. Take notes because you will need to refer this again. Believe me." He chuckled.

Pastor Brice broke it down plainly. In great detail, he explained that it is always best to identify the real root of the problem. If the issue is the lack of quality time being spent together then the argument should not be about toothpaste. He also gave explanation about the importance of effective listening skills, understanding that men and women handle issues differently, making time to deal with the issues—don't put them off and most of all, don't assassinate your spouses' character in an argument nor make them feel defensive. These were all really good tips for handling conflict resolution. I just hoped that if and when moments of disagreement arose, I could remember everything I learned.

"Pastor, those were some really good tips. Thanks." Zach smiled. "I learned a lot from your counsel. I feel like I could run out and marry Tori now."

"Awww, you don't have much longer, Zach. Just a few more days. It'll be here before you know."

"Well, I can't wait. Tori, you wanna elope?" Zach teased.

"Noooooooooooo way. After all we've put into this ceremony and reception, especially Mama? I don't think so, Mr. Ambrose."

"All right now, Tori," Pastor Brice said. "Remember it's not about the wedding. It's about the marriage. Many marriages fall short because more emphasis is put on the ceremony than the actual nuptials. Don't fall for the hype. I've known couples who have gotten married at the court house without all the glitz and glamour and had very successful marriages."

I hung my head in shame. Pastor was right. As many women do, they get caught up in the wedding and all the bells and whistles associated with it. I was guilty. "You're right, Pastor. Sorry."

"No need to apologize," confirmed Pastor Brice with his usual warm smile. "You two are a fine couple, and I have no doubt that this is a union God has put together. I'm proud of you both. You're a model couple—role models for the youth in the church. They look up to you and many, young and old, admire what you two share. You should be proud. God most definitely is please, and so am I."

I turned to look toward Zach who had seemed to be hit with a severe cough. "Honey are you alright?"

He nodded, but didn't speak. He was terribly choked up. This violent cough has totally taken over causing Zach to look like he could barely breathe.

"Are you sure?"

In a raspy voice, he responded, "Yeah, baby. It seems like something got caught in my throat. I'm okay now." He seemed to be struggling to recover from his cough attack.

Pastor Brice stood from his chair. "Zach, Tori. This is the end our sessions. I'm pleased to say you've done well. I'm sure if you continue to keep God first in your marriage, you will be fine. I have a good feeling about this union...a really good feeling. But, please know that when you hit those stumbling blocks or rough patches we discussed, my door is always open. Don't ever hesitate to come see me for anything—big or small. Do you understand?"

"Yes, Pastor," we answered in unison—Zach still not completely over his coughing fit. I wondered if he was coming down with something. I made a mental note to ask him when we left the church.

"Zach," Pastor Brice said, placing his hand on Zach's shoulder, "you've got a good, Godly woman here. Love her as Christ loved the church. Protect her, provide for her, encourage, nurture and support her at all times. Once you say 'I do', you become one."

Preparing myself for the send-off speech, I looked into Pastor's eyes as he turned to me. "Tori, you have a good, Christian, God-fearing man here. Continue to display Godly character and let God's light shine through you. Love him even when times are hard. Submit to him as you would Christ. Cherish him, support and encourage him and always show him affection. Got it?"

"Got it." I smiled.

"Good. Now, enjoy your last moments of single life, but ultimately prepare for the excitement of holy matrimony. Let's have a word of prayer before departing."

I looked over at Zach as I bowed my head to pray. He still looked a little uneasy. His face bore a combination of slight sadness and intense pain. He tried to mask his facial expressions when Pastor Brice would look at him, but I saw it all. He couldn't hide it from me. He needed to remember that I was a woman and a women's sixth sense was always on the alert. Zach wasn't fooling me. His demeanor said it all. He was ill—very ill. I could see it.

I continued to gaze at him with my head bowed and my eyes opened during the prayer. I eyed Zach. He appeared weak and flustered. Sweat beaded on his forehead. I noticed his palms felt clammy. He shifted his weight from one foot to the other. In essence, it looked like he had been hit with something out of the blue. But, what could've attacked his body in such a short span of time? He was fine earlier and now looked as if he was going to faint. Something was terribly wrong . . . horribly wrong, and before we left the church, I was going to get to the bottom of it.

Chapter 25

Mama

My bedroom was pitch-black and still. The only sound I heard was that of Norm breathing heavily. It was after midnight, but my eyes were wide-open as if it were twelve in the afternoon. I couldn't sleep. I had been trying for the past two hours, but sleep evaded me. I wish I could blame it on Norm's snoring, but it wasn't. The truth was that I had an uncomfortable feeling in the pit of my abdomen. I also had sharp pains shooting through my chest every so often. I couldn't easily identify the cause of what I was feeling, but I knew it was directly linked to my girls. Something wasn't right. Every fiber of my being told me there was something going on that I wasn't aware of. *But what?*

"Norm," I whispered, hoping he would hear me.

As much as I really didn't want to wake him, I needed to talk to somebody. I had been praying since my head hit the pillow, but a burden-like feeling still weighed heavily upon me. When Norm didn't respond, I spoke a little louder. "Norman," I called, reaching to tap his shoulder.

"Yeah?" he answered groggily.

"Baby, I'm sorry to wake you, but I can't sleep."

"What's wrong?" he said, turning over to face me.

"It's the girls. Something's not right. I can feel it. There's something going on that we don't know about."

"Aww, Janice. I think you're being paranoid. Things have been quiet with the girls for a while now. Tori's wrapped up into her upcoming marriage. Dani's been getting herself together and preparing to go back to work since the baby's death. Everything's cool. The girls are fine."

"They're not Norm. I tell you I can feel it. My gut tells me differently. And every time I think about them, I get this agonizing pain in my chest. The nightmares about the girls dying haven't stopped. Things aren't what they seem, Norm. My body and my subconscious mind are telling me so."

"Janice, you worry too much. You've got to learn to pick and choose your battles. I think you're so used to the girls fighting that when things settle down, you expect a big bomb to drop. Thank God there is finally some peace. You need it, they need it, and Lord knows I need it. Don't go borrowing trouble."

"You just don't understand, Nor—" I clutched my chest. Another razor-sharp twinge had come across my upper body, interrupting me mid-sentence. I could barely breathe. I was gasping for air.

"Janice," Norm called, sounding panicked. "Is it happening again?" I couldn't speak. I just nodded. "We need to get you to a hospital."

"No, no. I'll be all right," I spoke softly. "It comes and goes. This time it hit me a little harder than usual, but it always passes."

"I don't like this one bit. You've been complaining about these pains for weeks now. I'm telling you, woman, we're gonna see a doctor first thing in the morning. No ifs, ands or buts about it. Got it?"

I smiled slightly. Norm didn't put his foot down often, but when he did, I knew to never fight him on it.

"How are you feeling now?" he asked.

"Better. I told you it would pass. It always does."

"Yeah, well, we're still going to get you some medical attention ASAP."

"Well, Norm, let's just wait until after the wedding. All the planning and preparations could be wearing on me as well. I promise that as soon as we marry Tori off, I'll go to see the doctor."

"I don't think you should wait, Janice. I really don't."

"I'm sure I'll be fine, Norm. It's the girls. Y'all don't believe me, but they are breaking my heart. My chest never hurts unless I'm thinking about them. I'm not having nightmares about anything else but them. I'm not worried about anything else in this life but them. I've compared Dani and Tori's relationship to an Esau and Jacob conflict, but sometimes I fear it's going to be more of a Cain and Abel scenario. I don't want that outcome for my girls. I don't think I could survive the heartache of knowing one of my babies died at the hands of the other."

"Like I said before, the girls are fine. They aren't going to kill each other. At some point, you're just gonna have to let them live—whatever the outcome may be. You can't keep worrying about them, Janice. They're grown and appear to be happy with their lives. I know it's easier said than done, but you've got to stop carrying their problems, their issues. It's not healthy as you can see."

"You're right, Norm."

"Look at you—looking all sad. Your mouth says you agree with me, but I can tell your mind doesn't. Since I know you better than you know yourself, I know you need something to ease your mind right now. So, call'em up."

"Huh?"

"Call *your* daughters. That's the only way you're ever gonna get some sleep."

"But, it's late.

"So, what? Call them. For my sake and yours."

Norm was right. He knew me well. I really needed to talk to my babies just to make sure everything was all right. I hated calling them so late, but my heart and mind needed this.

I phoned Dani first. Surprisingly, she was not asleep. Said she was surfing the Internet while Kyle was asleep. I explained to her that I couldn't sleep because I had been up suffering from chest pains and worried about she and Tori. Dani assured me that nothing had been going on between she and Tori, that all things were well. I inquired about her mental health and she assured me that she was fine.

After hanging up with Dani, I called Tori. Unlike Dani, she was in a deep slumber. Initially, she assumed something was wrong, but I calmed her, by stating that I was just a little concerned about her and Dani, and I needed to hear their voices. She too, told me she was doing well and that there were no new issues between her and her sister.

Despite talking to both girls and hearing they were both doing well and there were no new, current beefs between them, I still couldn't shake the nasty gut feeling. Something wasn't quite right. But, since I couldn't put my finger on it, I decided to just take it to God in prayer. This time with a plan to leave it with the Lord and let Him handle whatever it was that was unforeseen to me.

Chapter 26

Tori

I couldn't get Mama off my mind all day. I was sitting with Denise, deep in reflection as thoughts of Mama weighed heavily upon me. Receiving that phone call from her last night really bothered me. To learn that she was still suffering from severe chest pain which seemed to be cause by Dani and me, distressed me greatly. My Mama meant the world to me and to know that she was enduring heartaches made me realize that I needed to change my attitude toward Dani. Even if she woke up everyday for the rest of her life hating me, I had to let go and let God. I for once had to be the bigger person—not for me, but for the sake of my Mama.

My silent contemplation was suspended when my telephone rang.

"Hello Kyle. What's up?"

"What are you doing?" he said abruptly.

"I'm sitting here with Denise, putting together my wedding favors. What's wrong with you? Why do you sound like you're out of breath?"

"I need to talk to you—NOW."

"About what?" I asked with a puckered brow.

"Don't want to get into that over the phone. I need to speak to you face to face."

"You're scaring me, Kyle. Tell me what's going on?"

"I'm on my way. I'm not far. I'll be there in two minutes." Click.

I took the phone from my ear, wondering what in the world was going on. Kyle sounded like he had just robbed a bank and needed somewhere to hide. His voice was that of edgy excitement and endless panting.

"What's going on with Kyle?" Denise asked.

"I don't know. He says he's on his way over to tell me. It doesn't sound good."

With a raised eyebrow, Denise queried, "Why is he coming to see you? You two have been awfully chummy lately. What's up with that?"

"Girl, please. Ain't nothin' going on with Kyle and me. For some reason, he's chosen me to be his confidant. I have no idea why."

"Hmmmmmmmmm, no idea why, huh? I bet I can tell you fifty million reasons why."

"Don't start, Denise," I teased. "I ain't even thinkin' about Kyle. Zachary Ambrose is my man, my fiancé, my future husband. Kyle doesn't stand a chance. He had his time, messed up and there is no going back for me."

"That's what your jaws are yapping. I'm not fully convinced. He's over here more than Zach. Why all of a sudden are you his shoulder to lean—"

Denise was interrupted by a loud banging on the door.

"My goodness," I said, startled. "Why is he pounding on my door as if his life is in danger?"

"Do you want me to leave? I mean, we can resume doing the wedding favors later if you'd like. I wouldn't want to be a third wheel, ya know?"

"Stop it, Denise! You sit your behind right there on that sofa and stay put. Kyle won't be here long. I promise you."

As I walked over to answer the door, I wondered what was so urgent. What had gotten Kyle all in a tizzy? I opened the door then addressed him.

"Kyle, what's going?"

He just brushed past me as if he didn't even see me standing at the door. When I turned to look at him, his body language screamed intense anger. His face was filled with fury. He looked as if he was a walking time bomb about to explode at any minute. I knew instantly whatever he had to tell me was serious. I looked over at Denise who appeared to be petrified by Kyle's fuming demeanor.

With a soft tone, I spoke. "Kyle, honey, what's the matter?"

"I knew it," he shouted. "I just knew it," he repeated, waving a manila envelope.

Slowly walking over toward him, I said, "You knew what?"

"I knew your sister was a lying, cheating, bitch. The gut doesn't lie, Tori. I knew it all along but didn't want to believe it."

"Oh, no. The private investigator actually found something?"

"Yes, indeed he did. I've got all the proof I need right here. She's been creeping for a minute."

"Say it ain't so, Kyle. I just don't want to believe it. I was really hoping that your assumptions about Dani were wrong." And that was true. I wanted Dani to be caught in her mess, but never wanted Kyle to be hurt in the process.

"Naw, they ain't never wrong, sweetheart. I was apart of the game. Game recognizes game. She must've thought I was some dumbass hood boy or something. That freak never expected me to be up on her mess. Now, I've got proof in black and white."

Still looking a bit uneasy, Denise spoke. "Tori, I think I should leave you and Kyle alone. This is private."

"No," Kyle bellowed. "Don't leave. Tori is gonna need you 'cause there's more."

I looked at him like he had three heads. *What in God's name was I gonna need Denise for? This had nothing to do with me.*

I was puzzled. "Kyle, what do you mean? I don't have nothing to do with this. This is really between you and Dani." My voice was trembling.

"Tori, girl, I love you to death. And by no means did I ever set out to hurt you when I started investigating Dani. I knew she was stabbing me in the back, but I had no idea she was doing the same to you."

"Kyle, what are you talking about?" I was becoming agitated. I needed Kyle to stop beating around the bush and just come out and tell me what he knew.

In a mellow tone, Kyle said, "I'm so sorry, Tori. I really am. But . . . but . . . but . . . the investigator discovered and gave me proof of Dani being involved with . . ."

"Who, dammit?" Stop procrastinating and say it. You're starting to piss me off, Kyle. Now with whom?"

"She's seeing Zach, Tori," he blurted. "She's having an affair with Zach, your fiancé."

Denise made a wheezing sound. She looked at me and then at Kyle..

I was totally confused by what Kyle had just said. So, I asked him to repeat it. "Run that by me again, Kyle. Dani's seeing who?"

With pain covering his face, Kyle said, "It's Zach, Tori. It's Zach."

"Kyle, bye," I yelled. "Time for you to go, buddy. Your time is up."

"You don't believe me?"

"Hell, no. Zach is my fiancé. The man I'm about to marry in a week. He loves me, Kyle. So, the last thing I would ever believe is that he'd be messing around with Dani. A whore like Dani is beneath him, Kyle."

Kyle didn't say another word. He just threw the envelope at me.

"What's this?" I asked.

"Open it?"

"What is this, Kyle?"

"I said open it," he snapped.

Now, my blood pressure was sweltering. I decided to open the envelope, so I could hurry up and get him out of my apartment and my life. I could only imagine he conjured up a lie about Zach just so he could have me back. If he thought, I'd come running back to him, he was sadly mistaken.

When I ripped the envelope, the contents revealed pictures— an abundance of pictures. I flipped through the stack of photos swiftly so I could get Kyle out the door. "Okay, Kyle, so there's a picture of Dani outside your house, at the mall, at the grocery store, at my parents house, outside of . . . wait a minute. Is this Zach's apartment complex?"

"Sure is. Keep looking."

I flipped through the photographs more vigorously. My heart literally sank when I saw pictures of Dani walking up to Zach's door, him answering the door in his boxers, photos of them kissing, images of him walking her to her car and leaning inside the car window kissing her, photos of them sitting in a parked car in the park; photos of him kissing her breast inside the car, photos of them holding hands, his hands around her waist, Dani sticking her tongue in his ear.

My hands fell numb. The stack of photos dropped from my hands onto the floor. I stood frozen and in shock. I couldn't fathom my Zachary, my fiancé, deceiving me all this time. I couldn't comprehend how he would be unfaithful to me with Dani. I was in utter disbelief.

"Tori, come sit over here," Denise said, ushering me to the sofa.

I sat without saying a word. I was in shock.

"Tori, say something, please. You're scaring me," Denise pleaded.

"Tori, I'm sorry, babe," Kyle mouthed. "I'm so sorry. I didn't do any of this to hurt you. I knew something was up with Dani but I had no idea it was Zach."

As Kyle spoke, the tears began to pour down my cheeks. Anguish immediately engulfed me. I fell from the sofa onto the floor wailing. "Noooooooooooooooooooo, God NO. Why, me Lord? Why me? Lord, what did I do to deserve this? What did I do? Why . . . why . . . why . . . can't I ever be happy, Lord. Whyyyyyyyyyyyyyy?"

Wrapping her arms around me, Denise said, "Tori, it's gonna be okay. God's got this, baby. God is all in this. Only a loving God would've allowed you to find out about Zach before making a lifelong commitment to him. Our Lord and Savior did you a favor, baby girl. He did you a huge favor."

I was listening to Denise, but I wasn't buying it. I was so hurt, angry and bitter that I allowed nothing she said to penetrate my brain. "That lying, cheating son-of-a bitch," I screamed. Now, I understand why he was all choked up, and sweaty-looking as if he was about to pass out at our last counseling session. He was full of guilt after Pastor Brice complemented us on being a model couple and role models for the youth in the church. That Negro knew all along he was full of manure. How could he do this to me? This man was supposed to me my husband, y'all. My husband."

"Denise is right, Tori. At least you found out before you married that joker," Kyle added.

"I hate him . . . I hate him . . . I hate him! The wedding is off. But somebody better start planning his funeral 'cause I'm gonna kill him." I jumped from the sofa, attempting to locate my car keys. I'd had enough of folks walking over me, using me, lying to me and stabbing me in the back. I was done. I created my own scripture, "Vengeance is mine, thus said Tori." I was out for blood and didn't care who I got to first. I was gonna murder somebody's child.

Kyle bolted over to me. "Where are you going?"

I growled, "To put someone to death."

"No, Tori, don't. You're way better than this. Dani and Zach aren't worth it. They ain't worth it."

I looked at him with disgust. "So, you think I'm just suppos-ed to sit here and cry all night. Hell naw. I'm gonna do something about it. I'm sick and tired of being the nice little church girl who everybody treats as a doormat. Fuck that!

I'm about to bring the pit bull out of me. These bastards are gonna pay for messing with me."

"What are you planning to do, Tori.?"

"Denise, I already told y'all. I . . . am . . . going . . . to . . . kill . . . them. Was that plain enough for you, or do you need me to spell it out?"

"I'm not letting you go anywhere. You're staying right here until you calm down. You're in no condition to drive."

"Yeah, Tori. I'm with Denise. You're not going out this door—not this upset."

"So, what y'all keeping me hostage in my own home?"

"No, Tori.," Denise spoke softly. "We just want you to calm down a bit. We understand you're hurt. We just need you to be a little more rational about this. I want to join you in kicking both their asses. I really do. But, I also know that two wrongs don't make a right. So, although they deserve whatever the hell they receive, I ain't trying to go to jail behind it."

"Tori, you know me well," Kyle spoke. "You know that it's taking every bit of restraint within me not to confront Dani right now. It would be nothing for me to go over to our house and strangle her or smother her with a pillow right about now, but I want to do this a different way. I want to fight Dani with her own artillery. If we're smart about this thing, we can get her and Zach in ways they'd least expect. So, let's take a minute to calm down and think this through."

"So, what are you suggesting, Kyle. If it's a good plan, I'm down. I've been sick and tired of Dani for years—since childhood and now Zach has just been added to my most wanted list. So, whatever is, I'm down."

I stared at Denise as she was co-signing with Kyle to get

revenge on Dani and Zach. This situation had brought out the worst in everybody, including my dear friend. I didn't know what had gotten into her, but I was loving it. The more on my team, the merrier.

As much as I hated to admit it, after seeing those pictures, all my Bible teaching, sermons I'd heard and chapters and verses I'd read meant nothing. I wasn't tossing them out my life for good, but I surely put the Word and God on the back burner for a minute. I was done being the fool. This time will be the last time. My sister the cum-bucket and my fiancé, the lying, piece of shit were going to wish they hadn't betrayed me.

Late afternoon the following day, I was awakened by the telephone. Zach called all the previous night and next morning. After ignoring his calls, I finally answered just to tell him I was ill. The conversation was brief. There was no need for me to put on an act because I was indeed ill, grief stricken and dismayed. I rushed him off the phone before he could utter more than a sentence. Just told him I needed to rest.

Kyle, Denise and I sat up until the wee hours of the morning, getting our plan of attack together. We just needed to put the finishing touches on everything but grew tired. Besides, my emotions were up and down. One moment I was overcome with sorrow, tears and snot running down my face and the next I was on the hunt for Dani and Zach's blood. I was as hype as Ice Cube in *Boyz in the Hood* when he wanted to avenge his brother Ricky's death.

When the phone stopped ringing, I looked over at Kyle who

was asleep on the floor next to my bed then at Denise who was asleep next to me in my bed. All the plotting had exhausted us, so I offered for both of them to crash at my place. Besides, I didn't want to be alone. I welcomed the company.

"Hey, Tori", Denise said rolling over. "Are you okay?"

"I'm hurting, Denise. I'm hurting. You don't know how bad I want to call and tell him the wedding is off. You don't know how bad I still really want to murder Zachary Ambrose. You just don't know."

"I empathize with you, sis, and honestly, I want you to do all those things with the exception of murder, but we have a great plan laid out. We're gonna get him where it hurts, honey. It's going to take both of them quite some time to bounce back from this. Look, I know it's hard, but we need you to stick to the plan. Stick to the plan, okay?"

I nodded. Denise and Kyle's methods were easier said than done. The wedding was in six days, and for six long days, I still had to play the happy, blushing bride-to-be. I had to go along with things as planned. Zach didn't have an inkling that things were over between us, but he'd find out soon enough. My parents were left in the dark. Pastor Brice had no idea of what had transpired. As far as everyone knew, Zachary Ambrose and Tori Prescott were getting married. Little did they know, I wasn't marrying Zach. Not in six days—not ever.

Chapter 27

Dani

"Hey, Dani. How are you, love?"

"Hi, Mommy," I responded, in a miserable tone.

"What's wrong with you? Why do you sound so sad?"

"I sound sad?" I asked, not realizing that my tone of voice matched the doom and gloom I was feeling.

"Yes, you do, baby? What's going on?"

"Nothing, Mama. I'm fine," I lied.

The truth: I wasn't fine. I felt absolutely wretched. In less than twenty-four hours, Zachary would be marrying Tori, and the thought of it made me nauseated. If ever I wanted a catastrophic event to occur, it was this day—or at least Tori's wedding day. I was hoping for a hurricane or tornado, hell even a terrorist attack—just anything to stop that wedding.

I had contemplated doing it myself, but I knew nothing good would come from it. I'd only add embarrassment and disgrace to Zach, my parents and myself. Still, I had been in deep thought as to how the marriage could be stopped. Somehow I needed to convince Mama that nothing was wrong before she started with twenty questions.

"If you say so, Dani. I believe there's more going on, but

I'll leave it alone for now. Anyway, I'm calling because I want to know if you're still planning to attend the wedding tomorrow?"

I sighed. As much as I wanted to stay at home clothed in pajamas, a scarf around my head and curled up in bed with a good book, I knew my mother wouldn't stand for it.

"Yes, Mama. I'll be there." I answered, while rolling my eyes.

I really didn't want to attend, but I knew Janice Prescott wouldn't let me hear the end of it, if I didn't. I had planned to be incognito in the back of the church. And as soon as the benediction was over, I would quickly disappear.

"Chile, you ought to be more excited. Your sister's getting married. That's a wonderful thing, don't cha think?"

"Mama, marriage these days ain't all it's cracked up to be. Marriage is a joke. People don't marry for love anymore. I don't believe marriages are made in heaven any longer."

Mama sounded perplexed. "Are you speaking in reference to yourself—your marriage or about Tori?"

"Both. My marriage is on the rocks. I haven't seen Kyle in five or six days. He's been staying with friends. He said he needs time away to sort things out, to determine if he still wants our marriage."

"Oh, no. Dani, I'm so sorry. What brought this on?"

"Mama, we've been having problems since the baby's death. It's been up and down between us for awhile."

"Why didn't you tell me? I could've been there for you."

"I know you would've, Mama, but I just wanted to handle it on my own. I believe Kyle and I will make it through this. I just figure it's a rough patch."

Truthfully, I was done with Kyle. We were married in name only. After he called me speaking in such a vicious, hateful tone, telling me he wasn't coming home, I decided that day there was no hope for us. I had come to think it was apparent Kyle couldn't let go of the past so we could move forward. Hell, I was halfway there myself. I was only willing to work on the marriage so it wouldn't appear to others that my farce of marriage failed. I wanted people, especially Tori, to believe Kyle and I were truly happy. In reality, he and I both were miserable. Neither one of us had a strong desire to repair the damage that had been done.

I prepared myself to move on, but I really wanted to move on with Zach, who was marrying, my evil twin sister. Surely something could be done to bring that wedding to a halt. But what? I searched my mind for things to do to prevent the ceremony but wasn't successful. I resorted to keeping my fingers crossed that something—anything would happen to bring Tori's joy to a standstill. Maybe Zach would come to his senses. I didn't know, but I was going to hold on to hope until they said, "I do". I heard Mama let out a deep sigh on the other end of the phone. I knew this not the news she wanted to hear.

"Dani, marriage is hard. Believe me, I know. You've got to work at it, honey. I hear defeat all in your voice, which means you've given up. If you love Kyle, you need to fight for him. Don't give into the devil. Don't give in to what society says about marriage."

"I hear you. I really do. But, it takes two. And if Kyle isn't willing, then there's nothing more I can do. I can't fix things by myself." I was doing a good job of convincing my mother that I really gave a damn about my marriage to Kyle. I didn't. The defeat she heard in my voice had everything to do with Zachary. That's all. Nothing more—nothing less.

"Look. We can talk more about this after the ceremony tomorrow. I have to tend to some last minute preparations. But, this is far from over. I am not going to let you throw in the towel yet. I'm gonna give you some old lady wisdom on how to keep your man." She chuckled.

"Okay, Mama. I'll be waiting to see what kind of mojo you're working with?"

"Mo—who?"

I laughed heartedly. "Nothing, Mama. Nothing."

"I love you, Dani. I'm praying for you and know that God is able to do exceedingly and abundantly above all things. So, if you put it in His hands, He'll see you through. You've got to come back to Christ, Dani. You've been out there trying to live life all on your own. Where has it gotten you? Nowhere. It's time to give Him some time, give Him your all, give Him the best that you've got and once you've done that, just sit back and watch Him work. He's the only way, my daughter. The only way. Now, think about what I've said. I'll be lifting you up in prayer."

"Thanks, Mama. I love you. I'll see you tomorrow."

"Love you, too. Bye-bye."

Mama never wasted a minute to preach me back to church. I wish her words brought about more conviction, but they didn't. Unless there was a wedding or a funeral, I had no intentions of ever going back to church or to God. The only thing I wanted so desperately was to be back in Zach's arms. To be in his arms just one more time, I'd simply give anything I had.

As the hour grew late, I prepared myself for bed. I needed to be mentally equipped to attend that wedding. Besides losing the baby, seeing Zach marry Tori was going to be one of the worst days of my life.

Chapter 28

Tori
The Wedding Day

I stood at the altar dressed as beautifully as any bride could ever be. My dress, although simple, was an elegant, white, satin, A-line gown adorned with a beaded trim neckline. But, as gorgeous as I may have looked on the outside, inside I was filled with turmoil. I stood at the altar next to this man whom I prayed for all my life—the man I thought God had intended to be my husband. I had overwhelming feelings of disgust and it took everything within me not to slap Zach as we stood in front of Pastor Brice. Every ounce of love I had for Zach was shriveled down to the size of a grain of rice the moment I was presented with evidence of his unfaithfulness—and with my sister of all people. That was simply unforgivable. I stared at Pastor Brice as he spoke so highly of Zach and me as a couple.

"I am so honored to have the pleasure of marrying two fine young people, Zachary Ambrose and Tori Prescott. They are indeed a model couple," Pastor Brice boasted.

I felt completely nauseated. *If only you knew, Pastor.* If only he was aware that the youth pastor of Brice Memorial was screwing my sister. If only he knew the youth pastor was a liar and a cheat. If only he knew that he was a fake and a phony. If only he knew.

The last few days leading up to the wedding hadn't been easy avoiding Zach. It was an even more difficult task not to blurt out what I knew about him and Dani when I'd spoke to him. But, I had to stick to the plan. According to Kyle and Denise, it was imperative not to go against what we'd set in motion. I told Zach that I didn't want to see him the last few days before the wedding. I gave him a song and dance about wanting us to really miss one another. Initally, he didn't agree with my plan, but ultimately gave into my wishes.

On my supposed wedding day, I stood in the sanctuary, before God, the church, our Pastor, friends and family next to a man for whom I harbored strong disdain, and little did anyone know, I was leaving out just as I entered—as Ms. Tori Prescott.

Pastor Brice continued to speak, "Before this lovely couple exchange their vows, they have a treat for those who share in their special day. Zachary and Tori have prepared a slideshow of their journey of love together. Let's praise God for this couple."

As the congregants applauded and shouted, "Amen" and "Hallelujah", the slideshow began. I stood stiff, preparing myself for all the drama that was about to unfold. K-Ci & JoJo, *All My Life*, lightly began to play as the introductory slide appeared which read: ZACHARY AND TORI'S JOURNEY OF LOVE.

Slide one was Zach and I on the beach in Miami. Slide two: Zach and I pictured at his birthday celebration held at the church. Slide three: Zach and I at the Inner Harbor. Slide four: Zach on bended knee proposing to me. Slide five: a tender kiss shared between Zach and me after I said yes to his marriage proposal.

I fought to hold back the tears as I watched the precious memories we shared. *How could he have done this me?* I loved him with my whole heart and with the blink of an eye, he sent my world crashing. To say I was heartbroken was an understatement. I was totally, completely devastated.

I continued watching, bracing myself for what was about to happen next. Slide six: a photo of Dani. Slide seven: a photo of Dani outside Zach's apartment building.

I immediately felt a shift inside the sanctuary. It was as if everyone, including Zach, wondered why photos of Dani entered *our* journey of love. I glanced over at Zach, and he seemed a bit anxious. He began shifting his weight from one foot to the other, but continued to hold his composure. Knowing what was about to come next, I glared at the theater screen.

Slide eight: a photo of Dani standing at Zach's front door with Zach dressed in nothing but boxer shorts.

Instantly, Zach turns to me and mouths, "What is this? What's going on?"

I smirked, "Keep looking."

Slide nine: Dani and Zach holding hands. Slide ten: Dani and Zach kissing. Slide eleven: Zach and Dani in a parked car, him kissing her breasts.

The audience gasped. My heart raced. Pastor Brice looked as if he'd seen a ghost. "Stop the show," he yelled. "Stop the slideshow now."

I heard Mama scream, "Lord, no."

An array of comments flooded the inside of the church from the on-lookers.

"Ut-oh.,"

"What in the world?"

"This can't be happening."

"Was that Zach with Dani?"

Zach turned to me with sorrowful eyes. Before he could speak, I yelled, "The wedding if off. I will not marry you today, tomorrow or ever. You are a liar, a cheat and full of deception. I hate you, Zachary Ambrose. I hate you!"

"Wait . . . wait," he said. "Those pictures have been fabricated. They're fakes, looks like someone photoshopped those images to make it appear as if I am having an affair with Dani and I am not! Somebody is tryin' to set me up. You've got to believe me baby. Please, baby, please—"

As I struggled to take off my engagement ring to throw down Zach's throat while he spoke, I heard a woman's voice from the back of the church amidst all the confusion.

"Don't beg her, baby. You don't need her." It was Dani, prancing her way down the aisle, working her way toward the altar. She stopped just in front of us. "Finally, you know the truth. Yes, Zach and I have been seeing each other for months," Dani bragged.

"Dani, stop this foolishness," Daddy shouted, making his way to the altar as well. I knew this had to be quite embarrassing for my parents to witness, but no one felt any worse than I did—no one.

"Naw, Daddy. It's time she knew the real deal," Dani said.

Sheepishly, Zach attempted to plead with Dani, "Please don't do this. Please."

"It's too late now," Dani insisted. "It's all out in the open for all to see. And once again, everybody and they mama can see I took your man. How ya like me now?"

Dani gave a hearty laugh.

And that's when I snapped. My vision became blurred. My body began to feel as if it had been invaded by something other than the Holy Spirit. As she continued to snicker in my face at the mess she created, I balled my fist, raised my arm, cocked it back as far as I could, and with great force, I punched Dani square in her face. Once the first punch landed, I didn't stop. Repeatedly, I punched her face as rapid and vigorous as a boxer hitting a punching bag. She attempted to fight back, but I must've been demon possessed. There was nothing she could do to me—nothing. She couldn't even begin to handle the slave-like beating I was giving her due to years of torment and backstabbing. Dani didn't stand a chance against the rage I had inside me. She simply couldn't.

The wedding attendees were further in an uproar, but that didn't stop me. Dani deserved that whipping, every prevailing blow that connected with her body.

In the midst of all the tumult, I heard Mama shouting, "Stop it . . . stop it . . . please stop it."

But I didn't. I felt Pastor Brice and Zach attempting to pull me off Dani. It didn't work. Dressed in my lovely wedding gown, I was prepared to go to jail. I wasn't going to stop hammering her head until she stopped breathing. My goal was to see her dead.

Then suddenly, I heard a loud, heart-wrenching shriek. I heard someone yell, "She fainted." This distracted me because

Dani was still attempting to defend herself against me. So, I knew it wasn't her that fainted. *So who*, I wondered.

In my moment of distraction, Kyle swiftly stepped between Dani and me, picked me up and carried me to the other side of the church. "Calm down, Tori. Calm down. You need to get yourself together. Your mother just passed out."

"My mother?" I said, panting. I was tired from beating Dani's ass.

"Yes," he said.

Without saying another word, I ran over to Mommy who was unresponsive, lying on the floor holding her chest. "Mama," I yelped. "Someone call an ambulance."

"Oh my God, Mama," I heard from behind me. It was Dani, finally discovering that Mama had fainted.

Before either of us could speak another word, Daddy who hovered over Mama's body, bellowed, "Get away! Both of you. This is all your fault. Get away from my wife. Just back away."

"But, Daddy," I pleaded.

"'But Daddy,' nothing. You and Dani caused this. Because of your foolishness, she passed out. You two are no earthly good, and I don't want you anywhere near my wife. Get away!"

I stood, and slowly backed away from Daddy. I had never, ever seen him so furious let alone speak to Dani or me in that manner. Feeling embarrassed, I disappeared into the crowd to find Denise and Kyle.

Shortly thereafter, the paramedics arrived, wasting no time getting Mama on the gurney and rushing her to the hospital. I hopped in the car with Denise, and we followed the ambulance. I cried during the entire drive because I suffered with agony as I replayed Daddy's irate words in my head over and over. My heart was indeed heavy, and I prayed all the way to the hospital. I prayed for God to forgive me for my actions, and most of all, to please be with my mama.

Chapter 29

Dani

Moments after Capri and I arrived to the University of Maryland Hospital's emergency room, Tori rushed in with Denise and Kyle in tow. I found it rather odd that Kyle had been sniffing up under Tori all day long. This made me wonder if he had anything to do with that fiasco at the church. I didn't put it past him, especially since he had been missing in action the past six days. I wouldn't have been the least bit surprised if he was spending those days helping Tori orchestrate that messy ass scheme. I planned to confront him on the matter later.

I grimaced as Tori rushed over to Daddy and asked, "How's Mama?"

He didn't respond. He merely walked away, leaving her dumbfounded. Inwardly, I laughed. The cold shoulder was exactly what she deserved after that ghastly wedding stunt she pulled. And just as I had planned to address the situation with Kyle, Tori was number one on my list. As soon as time permitted, I was going to finish what she started at the church.

We all sat in the ER, nervous with anticipation waiting to hear the status of Mama's condition. Capri was by my side, comforting me. While waiting Capri, tried to convince me to be seen by a doctor because of the injuries from the altercation with Tori. She said that I appeared to have a contusion on the left side of my forehead along with a split lip, and swollen eyes. I refused. I was more worried about Mama then I was myself.

I glanced over at Daddy who had been in constant prayer with Pastor Brice by his side. Then I peered at Tori who sat in the opposite corner of the ER waiting room with a tear-drenched face, being consoled by Denise and *my* husband. Not only was I pissed about Kyle but I was heated that her injuries were few, with minimal scratches on her face. She had to know that an ass-whipping was in her immediate future. Her bruises had to match mine, but first I needed to get an update on my mother.

Finally after what seemed to be hours, the doctor finally came into the waiting room to speak to Daddy. We all hurried to Daddy's side to hear the news.

Nervously, Daddy spoke. "Hi, Doctor. I'm Norman Prescott, Janice's husband. How is she?"

Shaking Daddy's hand, the doctor said, "Hi, Mr. Prescott. I'm Doctor Stewart." Then he paused and a grim look covered his face. "Sir, the prognosis isn't good."

We all gasped.

Dr. Stewart continued, "Mrs. Prescott suffered cardiac arrest, which is the abrupt loss of heart function. After careful assessment of the heart, it appears that she suffered from coronary artery disease. Because Mrs. Prescott wasn't treated within four to six minutes of her collapse, we are unable to reverse the damage done to the heart. Additionally, I had four other doctors examine Mrs. Prescott and her brain scan shows little to no activity. Her condition is critical. Currently, she's in a comatose state and is being kept alive by artificial life support. We'll continue to monitor her. Anything is possible, but at this juncture, you may want to consider how long you want to keep her on life support."

"Do . . . do . . . do you mean, there's no chance of recovery?" Daddy asked in a weak whisper. "That the only reason she is still alive is because of the machines?"

"Unfortunately, sir, that's true."

Instantly, a tear fell from Daddy's eyes. Tori screamed, "Oh no. Dear God, please."

I just fell numb. I couldn't digest the news or rather, I wouldn't allow myself to accept that my mother was dying. I just couldn't.

Before leaving the waiting area, Dr. Stewart compassionately said, "I'm so sorry, Mr. Prescott. My prayers are with you and your family. I'll give you some time to make any decision regarding the life support, but in the meantime, you and your family are welcome to go back to see Mrs. Prescott."

Solemnly, Daddy said, "Thank you, doctor," as he wiped the tears from his face with his handkerchief.

Capri walked over to me and wrapped her arms around me. I was distraught by the news. "Oh, Dani. I'm so sorry," she cried.

"Not my Mama, Capri. Not my Mama."

I turned from Capri's embrace to see Tori crying in Kyle's arms. Instantly, my sadness turned into anger. "This is all your fault," I yelled across the waiting room at Tori. "All your fault. Had you not pulled that slideshow mess at the wedding, none of this would've happened. Now *my* mother is dying because of you."

"Listen whore," Tori retorted, "Had you not been sleeping with my fiancé, there would have been no need for a slideshow to expose your low-down dirty, lying, scheming ass. So, before you go blaming me, you need to take a long look in the mirror."

"For the love of God, please shut up," Daddy yelped. "My wife, your mother is dying, and all the two of you can do is argue? Don't you think both of you have caused enough damage? Why don't you grow up and act like women for once in your lives? You two have been acting like dysfunctional idiots for years, and quite frankly, I'm fed up. If you can't come together now and put your petty differences aside at a critical time such as this, then I don't want you here. Leave. Go. Just leave my presence." Daddy continued to weep as he scolded us. "The sight of you two bickering fools is making me sick. So, go on. Get out. Let me have some peace as I prepare to make the most difficult decision of my life—removing my precious wife from life support and ultimately watching her die. Just go. I don't want you here."

Before either one of us could say another word, Pastor Brice, grabbed me by one arm and Tori by her arm then roared, "I need to speak with both of you now. Let's go!"

Chapter 30

Tori

Pastor Brice swiftly escorted Dani and me into a small conference room down the hall from the ER waiting room. When we walked in, he closed the door behind us and firmly said, "Have a seat." We did, sitting on opposite sides of the conference room table. "Dani and Tori, I've known you all your lives, and I must say I have never been so disappointed in your vile actions. Do you understand the doctors just announced that your mother is basically dead? If there is no brain activity, that means she's brain dead. If the brain isn't functioning, nothing else in the body can function." He stopped briefly to look at us. I guess he wanted to see if his words were getting through to us. "The only reason your mother is still considered among the living is because she's connected to machines. Once the tubes are removed and the power switch is turned to off, your mother will die. Can either of you comprehend this? Can you?" he asked sternly.

Neither of us responded. Instead we wept and continued to listen to the pastor lecture us on our horrible behavior.

"Your father doesn't need this right now. He's hurting. He's been married to your mother forever. They have been inseparable. So, for him to abruptly be without her is undoubtedly killing him. You two are the closest he has right now and unfortunately, the two people he has to count on throughout this entire ordeal are only adding more strife and angst to this already grim situation. What will it take for the two of you to let this bitterness and hatred go? What good has come from all this back and forth, viciousness and backstabbing? How are either of you edifying God with this malicious behavior? What joy did you bring to your parents today with that horrible display put on at the church? Nothing. This is senseless and unnecessary and needs to stop—NOW. As God is my witness, if the two of you can't make amends for your dying mother, then I'll happily escort you out of this hospital because you will not hurt Brother Norman in the midst of all of this. Now the choice is yours."

There was silence. Neither Dani nor I spoke. Dani grabbed a tissue from the box on the conference room table and dabbed her eyes. I held my hands to my face and continued sobbing.

"While you're sitting here, hopefully letting my words sink deeply into your thick skulls, I will fill you ladies in on one of the last conversations I had with your mother. Of course, as the pastor of Brice Memorial, your mother and I were very close. She's talked to me for years about your relationship or lack thereof. And time after time after time, I've encouraged her and attempted to uplift her pertaining to this. Just before the wedding, when we spoke, I could tell she felt defeated. Sister Prescott described a feeling deep within her soul that she couldn't shake. She explained calling you both late one night when she couldn't sleep and her heart was filled with pain. It seems that you girls assured her that things were fine between the two of you, but after your recent display of contemptible behavior at the church, her feelings were on target. You two have no idea how tormented Sister Prescott was by your tumultuous relationship. She felt as if God wasn't ever going to answer her prayer about her twin babies having a healthy relationship. Right before the wedding, she was eagerly decorating the church. You all know how she loved putting on a wonderful display for events and for her daughter's wedding, she was sure to go above and beyond to make the atmosphere spectacular."

I managed to crack a smile when I thought back on how Mama loved planning events. That was truly her passion. I knew not to even get in her way, when it came to planning my wedding because I knew she wasn't having it. I continued to listen to Pastor Brice.

"During our conversation, she said, 'Pastor, if I could have one wish before God calls me home, it's for my daughters to form a sibling bond. I'm not asking for them to be best friends, but at least learn to respect each other—at least learn how to coexist in the same environment without the room being laden with contempt and hostility. Pastor, honestly, my heart can't take this pain anymore. If God never does anything else for me, I'd hope he'd grant me one last wish before leaving this earth and that is for Dani and Tori to come together as sisters. It's that simple. Am I asking too much?'"

After hearing Pastor Brice describe his last conversation with Mommy, I couldn't stop the tears from pouring. The guilt was insurmountable. I had no idea how much anguish I caused my Mama for so many years. Pastor's lecture didn't stop there.

"You should be ashamed of yourselves for putting your mother through that turmoil day after day, month after month, year after year. I mean, really. When I look at you two, I see classy, warm, engaging young women, but when the two of you are in the same room, you change. You become cold, still and withdrawn. How can either of you allow the other to have that much control over your character? How can you allow each other to force you to stop being who you are to turn into small, petty, ugly-spirited people? Dani, when you react to something Tori has done, she's gained control over you. Tori when you react negatively to something Dani's done to you, she's gained control over you. If you two were truly who you professed to be, Dani, Ms. Educated, and Tori, Ms. God-fearing Christian, then no one could hammer you down and change the person you are."

Pastor Brice was pounding on us something terrible. He wasn't holding back either. I didn't know about Dani, but he surely was making me feel like the size of an ant. I was extremely mortified to be getting reprimanded by the Pastor.

"Listen, girls. Have you all suffered enough losses in your life? Dani, with you losing the baby, and Tori, with the loss of your relationship with Zach, and now your Mama. Aren't you tired of suffering? Now I sit here and I watch both of you, full of tears and remorse, so I'm telling you that you must get down to business for time is not on our side."

"One of you", Pastor Brice said pointing at both of us, "has to be the conqueror in this situation. One of you has to be willing to throw in the towel, say enough is enough. You're playing with fire, and one of you has to be willing to step up to heal this situation. There comes a time when you have to be above the resentment and the bitterness because the stakes are high, lives are hanging in the balance—including your own. God isn't pleased and neither is anyone else. There's no greater gift you can give your mother at this critical time than to know that her daughters have claimed some peace."

"Pastor," I tearfully spoke, "I fully understand where you're coming from, and I agree with you, but you've got to realize that there's been so much damage done and the emotional scars are deep. It's going to be hard to overcome."

"Yeah, Pastor," Dani chimed in. "The antipathy between Tori and me didn't just happen over night. There has been years and years of hurt endured."

"Look. I hear where you girls are coming from. I am aware that there is some unfinished emotional business that we cannot fix today. Counseling is definitely needed, and I'm willing to help with that, but right now, we don't have time to find a suitable counselor. I need, no let me rephrase, your mother and father need you to do something today. I know the journey to love and forgiveness is a difficult one. I'm not asking you to love each other today. I'm asking that you start the journey by stopping the hate—for your mother, the woman who displayed unwavering love for the both of you. We can make this first step right here and now. Can you just look at each other and say this simple phrase: "I'm sorry."

Dani stood. She took two deep breaths and mouthed, "I can't, Pastor Brice. Not right now."

Before Pastor Brice could respond, Dani swiftly left the conference room and slammed the door behind her.

Emotionally drained from the events of the day, I gently lay my head on the long, wooden table and closed my eyes.

"Tori, I'll be right back. Let me see if I can find Dani."

"It's no use, Pastor. No use."

Chapter 31

Dani

"Dani! Dani!" Pastor Brice called. I continued to walk quickly, ignoring him as he bellowed my name.

"Dani, wait," he said winded as he caught up to me. "Please don't leave. We were making great progress. I felt a breakthrough. Don't give up on us now."

"Like, I said. I can't do this. Too much damage has been done. Tori is the devil, Pastor. She puts up a good act for you. I know I have many issues, but at least I don't front like I'm the golden child and act another way when the church-folk aren't watching."

"I understand the scars are profound. I'm not denying that, however, I think now is the time for healing. The tumultuous relationship that you and Tori have had hasn't gotten you anywhere. Nothing good has come from the arguing and fighting. Now, both of you are facing, undoubtedly one of your biggest fears—the loss of a parent. This is not a time for division. It's time to put differences aside and come together for your parents."

"I hear you. I really do, but I need more time."

"You may not have the time you seek, but I'll let you be for now. Think about what I've said."

Pastor Brice walked away from me with a look of disappointment. In my heart, I knew he spoke the truth about Tori and me, but I couldn't bring myself to forgive her for all she's done. No one seems to remember that she was the same person who drove me to attempt suicide. And most recently she had those impure pictures of me with Zach on display for all the wedding attendees to see. Our family, friends, friends of friends, neighbors, church members, colleagues and a host of other people witnessed the fiasco. At the time the slide shows were being viewed, I was angry, revengeful but now I am embarrassed. Nothing I've ever done humiliated Tori in public, however, she succeeded in making me look like an adulterous whore in front of hundreds of people. Others may be able to overlook her hatefulness, but I couldn't.

I strolled down the brightly lit hospital hallway heading toward Mama's room. Upon entering, my eyes met my daddy's red, puffy eyes. He looked weary.

"Hey, Daddy. How's Mama?" I cautiously asked. I knew he was still furious with Tori and me.

His response was direct. "No change."

"Do you mind if I sit with her for a few minutes?"

He gave me a look of hesitancy as if he didn't want me anywhere near Mama. "You can stay as long as you leave the negative energy at the door." He warned.

"I promise, daddy. I just want to be by her side for awhile."

Daddy exited the room without saying another word.

I pulled down the rail on the right side of Mama's hospital bed. I slowly sat beside her and grabbed her hand. My heart ached to see my mother in a state of lifelessness. I glanced at the IV needle stuck in her hand, the breathing tube nestled in her mouth, and the endless wires coming from her body. The room was cold and still. The only noises heard were the beeping sound coming from the life sustaining machine which was loud and steady. This moment seemed so surreal. Like something I'd only seen in movies.

Softly, I began talking to my mother. "Mama, I don't know if you can hear me but I want you to know how sorry I am. I didn't mean to hurt you like this, Mama. I was so caught up in me, me, me that I didn't care how my actions affected those around me. I love you, dearly. I really do and I'll do whatever it takes for you to come back to me. Anything. Just wake up right now and tell me what it is you want and I'll do it. I promise."

I sat quietly waiting for my mother to open her eyes. She didn't. I was dismayed. My gut told me that my mother's spirit may be leaving her body soon.

"Mama," I said with waterfalls coming from my eyes. "Pastor Brice said that you had one wish before God calls you home and that was to see your twin babies form a bond. Is that true, Mama? If I put aside my differences with Tori, would that make your heart better? Is that all you really want, Mama? Is it?"

I felt a slight squeeze on my hand. I was startled a bit. I looked at Mama's face which showed no change, no signs of life. I figured what I felt was just my imagination until I felt it again. This time a tighter, long grip. I continued to hold on to her hand until she gradually released her grasp.

As much as I wanted Mama squeezing my hand to mean she was awakening from her coma, I knew that it was sign for me to grant her final wish.

Still very much on edge about making peace with Tori, I knew I had to rise above the resentment and anger for Mama's sake.

I gave Mama a gentle kiss on her forehead. I raised the bed rail and quietly left the room. When I walked toward the waiting room, Daddy who had been sitting with Pastor Brice and Tori jumped from his seat and hurried to return to Mama's room.

"Feeling a little better, Dani after visiting with your mother?" Pastor Brice questioned.

"A little." I whispered.

"Do you want to finish our talk?"

"Ignoring his question, I asked, where is Capri?"

He answered, "She, Kyle and Denise went to the cafeteria for beverages. Would you like something?"

"No, sir. I'm fine. I have to run to the restroom. I'll be right back." Before Pastor Brice could protest, I scurried down the hall in the direction of the ladies room. "Damn," I blurted as I locked myself in the stall. I was so closed to granting Mama's wish but something in me still couldn't release the resentment.

I sat on the toilet seat, fully clothed with my face buried in my hands. I was overcome with anxiety. I broke into a sweat. The thought of reaching out to Tori was foreging to me. As much as I wanted to do this for Mama, I couldn't. I just didn't have that conqueror spirit in me to begin the healing process with Tori. I just couldn't.

Chapter 32

Tori

"See, Pastor Brice. I can't do this by myself. If Dani isn't willing to work with me on reconciliation, then it won't happen."

"Don't give up just yet Tori. God hasn't had the final say-so on the matter. Besides, I can see Dani softening. Something happened in the room with your mother. We'll never know the details, but I know something did."

With my mind full of doubt, I replied, "I'm glad you're still holding out hope because I'm not. I know her, Pastor. Mama being on her deathbed ain't going to change nothing. Dani is still gonna be Dani regardless.'

"Hush your mouth. I won't have you sit in my presence and doubt the power of the Lord. Like I said, it ain't over until God says it's over."

Pastor Brice was obviously still quite annoyed with me. So, I shut my lips tightly and didn't speak again until Denise returned with my bottle of apple juice.

"Any updates?" Denise asked.

"Nothing new," daddy responded walking up behind Denise. "The doctor came in about five minutes ago and asked if we had made any decision yet. I told him I hadn't but would consult with the family."

As daddy informed us of the doctor's most recent visit, Dani entered the conversation and said, "What are you gonna do daddy?"

He shrugged. "I don't know. I can't think straight. It would be nice to have my girls to lean on right now, but since you two are probably still bickering, I will make the decision on my own. I'm going back to be with Janice now." Daddy walked away with his head hung low. It was devastating seeing him look so bewildered.

When Daddy walked away, Pastor Brice beckoned Dani and me back to the conference room. "Look. I am not going to keep pleading with you girls all night. Time if of the essence. Your mother needs you. Your father most definitely needs you. So, I'll say this again. With my help, you can make the first step toward healing your relationship. It's not gonna be easy, but it can be done. Now, can we put aside the past and come together for the sake of your mother? Which one of you is willing to make the first stride towards healing?

Pastor Brice didn't have to say another word. He no longer needed to preach, beg or plead with me to make amends with my sister. It was the right thing to do. It was the Christian thing to do. It was the ultimate sacrifice I could make for my mother. So, without a second thought, I stood from my chair and walked over to where Dani sat. When I approached her, I sorrowfully said, "Dani, I'm sorry." I extended my hand with the hope, she'd be willing to shake on it and call a truce.

Dani didn't respond right away. She just sat there staring into space as if she didn't see me standing or heard my apology.

"Dani?" Pastor Brice called to her. "Did you hear your sister?"

"Yes . . . yes I did," she gently spoke. "But I don't want to shake her hand."

Dani's comment seemed to have shocked Pastor Brice and me. I thought after all the lecturing we could at least temporality make amends.

"Pastor, I don't want to shake her hand . . . but . . . but . . . but I'd like to give her a hug if she'd allow me."

Dani stood from her chair and wrapped her arms around me with a mighty hold. I squeezed her back. Our embrace was warm and genuine. I didn't want to let my sister go. I wanted to hold on to her for eternity because I was afraid the peace and truce could abruptly come to an end. The water that flowed from our eyes was non-stop. This was truly a moment we both cherished. It felt like God had rehabilitated our sibling bond.

"Oh hallelujah," Pastor Brice rejoiced. "Thank ya, Lord. Thank ya!"

After a few moments passed, Pastor Brice took a moment to pray over us while we held each other tightly. And after his prayer, he said, "Come on, ladies. Let's go see your mama."

Chapter 33

Dani

Hand in hand, Tori and I eased into Mama's hospital room with Pastor Brice following. Daddy was at Mama's bedside, holding her hand with his head gently resting on her forearm. Tori and I walked over to the opposite side of Mama's bed. I called to him.

"Daddy," I tenderly spoke.

He slowly raised his head, which revealed bloodshot eyes. He immediately looked surprised to see Tori and me standing side by side, with our hands intertwined.

"Daddy, we're so sorry," Tori said. "We've behaved like complete fools, but with the help of Pastor Brice, we've finally seen the error of our ways. From this day forward we've vowed to work out of differences and come together just like you and Mama have always wanted."

"That's right, Daddy," I chimed in. "We're starting our journey to forgiveness today."

"Are you serious?" Daddy questioned.

"Yes, Brother Prescott," Pastor Brice interjected. "I can't tell you it was easy with these two, but after some time, a long talk and divine intervention, they have agreed to work toward healing their relationship."

Daddy smiled slightly. "I love you, girls. You've made me and your mama so proud." Then he looked at Mama compassionately. "See Janice. I told you there was nothing to worry about. Our girls have finally sought peace. Come on, Janice. You've got to praise God with me one last time."

I leaned down to whisper in Mama's ear. "Yes, Mama. We did it. We did it, Mama. Just like you always prayed for. I'm regretful it took so long and under these circumstances, but your girls have finally come together." I truly hoped she could hear me.

"Mama," Tori said. "I, too, apologize from the bottom of my heart for all the pain, agony and sleepless nights I've caused you. You didn't deserve it, and if I could take it all back, I would."

Just as Tori leaned down to kiss Mama's cheek, Dr. Stewart entered the room. Daddy looked at him and nodded. Startled by the unspoken message between the two, I asked, "What's going on, Daddy?"

With a voice full of grief, Daddy whispered, "I made the decision a little while ago. Janice would have never wanted to be kept alive in this manner. She valued quality of life. Therefore, I won't prolong her earthly stay any longer. So, now it's time. It's time."

"No Daddy. Does this have to be done right now?" I fearfully asked.

"Yes, Dani. It's time to give your mother rest—wonderful, sanctified rest with our Lord."

"No, no, no, Daddy. Not yet," Tori sobbed. "Not yet. I need more time."

Dr. Stewart paused after hearing Tori's pleas. But, Daddy nodded again giving him the go ahead.

We gathered closely around Mama as Dr. Stewart began the process of unhooking Mama's life support. At this time, Pastor Brice walked over to the bed and said, "Let us pray. Dear Heavenly Father, with heavy hearts we come to You. You are the Almighty Creator God; holy and full of grace and love. The weight of our hearts is profound because of a life that is leaving us. Death engulfs us Lord. Fear is waiting to take us down, but we lay fear at your feet. Take the hand of our dear wife and mother, Janice Prescott and make Yourself known.

"Lord, we are before You, confessing that You are Lord of all; the gate keeper to eternal life. Your promise is that You will come to take us home. As it says in Psalm 23:4: *"Even though I walk through the valley of the shadow of death, I will fear no evil, for you are with me; your rod and your staff, they comfort me."*

I ask that you allow this family to bask in the comfort we find in Your presence. Send the Prescott Family Your peace Lord; the peace that passes all understanding. Don't let them waiver and doubt. Don't let them grow bitter in this shadow of death. But penetrate their hearts with a joy that we can not fathom or understand. Give them a faith that is everlasting. As they wait and watch, we know, Lord, that none of us will escape this journey through death. Teach them how to embrace it with faith.

"Father, please comfort as their grief seems to over power them and help them to understand that it's a grief and a mourning that holds joy on the other side. You are conqueror of all; and so we trust You. We trust that You will do what is right, what is loving. Whether in death or in life Your will is accomplished and You are sovereign. In the name of Jesus we pray, Amen."

After Pastor's prayer, Tori and I kissed Mama and repeatedly told her how much we loved her. We both laid our heads upon her chest and within minutes, she took a deep breath and the heart monitoring machine flat-lined. She was gone. Our mother was dead.

Hurt and sorrow couldn't begin to describe the emotions that flooded Mama's hospital room. Pastor Brice continued talking to God as he was filled with sadness. Kyle, Denise and Capri stood sobbing as they realized that life had left Mama's body. Daddy, stricken with grief, came over to embrace Tori and me. "Oh, Daddy," I cried. "Do you think she knew? Do you think she knew Tori and I had made peace?"

Daddy managed a smile. "Look at her face. Doesn't she look peaceful? She left this earth with a serene look spread across her face. She knew, baby. She knew. Believe me, everything is well with her soul."

Epilogue

Tori

One Year Later

"Hey, Mama," I sang. "It's your two favorite girls."

It was the one year anniversary of Mama's death, and Dani and I decided to visit the cemetery to put fresh flowers on her grave. We both sat at the foot of her tombstone to have a little talk with her, catch her up on our lives.

"Mama, I don't know why we felt the need to update you on our lives," I told her. "Although you aren't physically here with us, we still feel your presence. Mama, we know you're looking down from heaven, covering us, still being our mama."

"But just in case you missed anything," Dani said, "we still wanna update you, especially since we have some good news. Tori and I are still making you proud. We have continued our journey to healing, and it's been great. I never knew what I was missing not having my sister as an active part of my life."

"Yeah, Mama, Pastor Brice set us up with a wonderful Christian counselor who has been phenomenal in helping us work through the emotional scars and teaching us how to move forward."

Dani chimed in, "And Mama, I know you longed for me to get back into therapy for my Bipolar disorder and I have. I am also proud to say that I am regularly taking my medication again."

I glanced at Dani and said, "Don't you have something you wanna tell Mama?"

"What?"

"You know—about that one Sunday in church."

"Oh, that. Guess what, Mama? I gave my life to Christ a few Sundays ago. Yep, Mama, I finally confessed with my mouth and truly believe in my heart that Christ is Lord."

"Isn't that a blessing, Mama? Your daughter ain't a heathen no more." We both fell into laughter. It felt good to laugh with my sister.

"Nope, Mama. I'm not a heathen anymore, but I am single again." A look of sudden sadness crossed Dani's face. "Kyle filed for divorce soon after your funeral. I guess I missed out on that talk you had in store for me as to how to keep my husband. He's now dating some other woman, and I'm all alone."

"Hey, hey, now. Don't be looking all defeated. I'm still single, too, and that's fine with me. But, Mama, ain't nothing wrong with being the Prescott girls, is it? As long as we've got God, Daddy, each other, and you looking down on us, we don't need nobody else."

I sincerely meant every word I said to Dani. After the horrible way things ended with Zach, I began to focus on me—attempting to better my life and to renew my relationship with my sister. As hard as it was to fathom initially, I had finally forgiven Zach. Shortly after Mama's passing, I received a letter from Zach expressing his sincere apology for how he'd hurt me. He had also resigned as youth pastor at Brice Memorial as well as his membership and requested a transfer to work at another school. I never responded to Zach's letter or attempted to reach out to him, but in my heart I had forgiven him.

As for Kyle, I hadn't spoken to him much since his divorce from Dani. He and I remained distant friends. After throwing it up in Dani's face that he had her investigated, he all but spit in her face before totally walking out on her. And because he still harbored lots of resentment toward Dani, he and I couldn't see eye to eye on the forgiveness issue.

"Oh, and Mama. Let me tell you about Daddy," Dani laughed. "I think he's sick of us. We are always at the house, smothering him. When he sees us coming through the door, he looks like, 'not you two again.' It's too funny, Mama. He tries to play the tough role, but he knows he loves our daily visits. So, don't worry about Daddy. We are suffocating him with our attention and love."

I grinned at the thought of Daddy. He seemed to be managing pretty well over the past year. Of course, sometimes I'd see a look of loneliness in his eyes, but I believe it's his faith in God that's sustained him. He also remained active in the community and at church. And whether he liked it or not, he was stuck with us.

"Well, Mama, we're gonna be leaving now, but we'll be back before you know it. We've enjoyed our talk with you. It is our greatest hope that you are proud of the women we've become and that we continue to bring a smile to your face up in Heaven— something we were unable to do while you were here with us on Earth. For that Mama, I sincerely apologize."

Epilogue

Dani smiled. "Me too, Mama. Me, too." Kissing Mama's headstone, Dani mouthed, "Love you, Mama."

Sliding my hand across the top of her headstone, I said, "I love you, too, Mama."

As Dani and I turned to walk away from Mama's resting place, I reached out and took her hand. "I love you, twin."

"I love you, too, twin."

It was always hard leaving the cemetery after a visit with our precious mother, but *this* time, I was certain that Dani shared the exceeding joy I had in my heart, knowing that our lives and sisterly bond had been renewed in God's love.

Notes

Notes